ABOUT THE AUTHOR

Norman Dannatt

Norman started his career in Wartime ENSA as a professional musician in the theatre. He had trained as a performer (piano, organ, sax, clarinet and percussion), and, after the War, became a composer for many shows in London's West End theatres. Then, after training as a teacher, he taught in secondary, junior and infant schools. For the last 11 years until he retired, he was School Inspector for Music to the London Borough of Havering. Since retirement he has continued working as a part-time lecturer in music education and as a consultant to several musical instrument firms, including, of course, The Clarke Tinwhistle Company. He can even play the Tinwhistle. A bit!

He wishes to express his thanks to contributors for the first and second editions and asks anyone who reads this book and has anything more to add, no matter how trivial, to write to him, c/o The Clarke Tinwhistle company, for him to add it to a possible third edition.

Norman Dannatt

THE HISTORY OF THE
TINWHISTLE

The story of Robert Clarke and his famous Tinwhistle
1843 to the present day

*To Dave Seward
with thanks for your help
Norman Dannatt*

First edition published in Great Britain by
The Clarke Tinwhistle Company Limited
in 1993

This revised edition published in 2005 by
Corunna Publications
10 Corunna Close
Hythe
Kent CT21 5EA
Great Britain

ISBN 0-9549693-2-4

© Norman Dannatt 2005

Norman Dannatt is hereby identified as author of this work in accordance with Section 77 of the Copyright, Designs and Patents Act 1988.

All rights reserved; no part of this publication may be reproduced or transmitted by any means, electronic, mechanical, photocopying or otherwise, without the prior permission of the publisher.

Design by Moffitt Design

Printed in Great Britain by
Opasco Limited
9-17 Crompton Way
Crawley
West Sussex RH10 9QG

The Clarke Tinwhistle Company Limited
The Old Joinery
Whetsted Road
Five Oak Green
Tonbridge
Kent TN12 6RS
Great Britain

telephone: +44 (0)1892 837433
fax: +44 (0)1892 837434
email: norman@clarketinwhistle.com

Contents

7 Acknowledgements

9 Foreword

11 Introduction

13 Robert Clarke and his family

33 The Weedons

41 The Making of a Clarke Tinwhistle

61 Whistlers Past and Present

91 Envoi

Acknowledgements

I would like to extend my grateful thanks to the following, who have helped me in the preparation of this book:-

Alan, Fred and Keith Clarke, great grandsons of Robert Clarke; Harry Tomlinson, husband of Doris, great granddaughter of Robert Clarke; Joan Sandilands, great granddaughter; Angela Small and Janice Clarke, great great granddaughters of Robert Clarke, for giving me family history material.

The great Irish tinwhistle players, Mary Bergin, Tommy Makem, Micho Russell, and Michael Tubridy for giving me information about themselves and their playing of the Clarke Tinwhistle. The American, Les Lieber; the Scotsman, Will Hastie; the Englishmen, Des Lane and Tim Moon and the New Zealander, Dr. Roger Buckton for being equally helpful.

Bill Ochs, tinwhistler; author of *The Clarke Tinwhistle*, the definitive Handbook and Tutor; and proprietor of the Pennywhistler's Press, for information about himself and many famous tinwhistlers.

Brian J. Laline, Editor of the *Staten Island Advance* and Steve Zaffarano, photographer, for permission to use Mr. Zaffarano's photograph of Bill Ochs.

Nigel Schofield, erstwhile Editor of *Tyke's News*, for permitting me to reproduce an article from his magazine.

Philip Hirst, Editor of the *Oldham Evening Chronicle*, for permitting me to reproduce extracts from his newspaper.

The National Trust of Northern Ireland for giving permission to feature the photograph of James Galway.

Dave Sewart of the Arthur Ransome Society for getting me a photo of Arthur Ransom playing his Pennywhistle and giving me information about the Arthur Ransome Society.

Foreword

I am not really a musician. To claim to be one would be an injustice to real musicians. But, I love music and I am a frustrated pianist, flautist, oboist, guitarist, concertina player, etc. etc. Also, for much of my life, I have tended to not have quite enough disposable income to buy a good instrument of any type. So, I've long had an interest in making music with inexpensive instruments.

So it was with this disposition and history that in 1994 or 1995, I forget which, I visited Bob Tedrow's musical instrument shop in Homewood, Alabama, near where I live. Bob specializes in a range of acoustic instruments and has since become best known for making fine concertinas. On a shelf in his shop I found a cardboard box filled with tinwhistles. I had just heard Joanie Madden, the great flute and whistle player, interviewed on the radio talking about this instrument. I bought an unpainted Clarke tinwhistle in D. Bob told me everything he knew about the instrument, which wasn't that much.

I tucked this unassuming little instrument into the sun visor of my minivan and started noodling around with it during my daughter's interminable and numerous soccer practices. At some point, I reached a critical threshold. I suddenly became fascinated, even a bit obsessed, with the instrument. To shorten this story a bit – and some readers

will be muttering that it is too late for that – I started researching the instrument, ordering different makes and models, and put up a simple little website on the Internet. I put my email address on the bottom of the website. I started hearing from people worldwide who played the instrument and who had stumbled on the website. From those weird and humble beginnings, Chiff & Fipple, the very large and busy online community devoted to the weird and humble tinwhistle, was born.

I retain a great fondness for the Clarke instruments. I visited the factory in Kent, England as the guest of my friend, the author of this book, Norman Dannatt. The Clarke goes back to 1843 and the 21st century model does not differ fundamentally from the design of the 1843 model. A piece of tin, rolled around a metal mandrel, then fitted with a wooden block, made and hand-voiced in England. Now there are many makers of tinwhistles, including handcrafted instruments made from silver, African blackwood, all kinds of woods and metals and plastics. These can cost as much as 100 times the cost of a new Clarke. And yet, to my hands and ears, the humble Clarke whistle retains a charm and a playability that I would never want to give up.

And what to say about the new edition of this indispensable little book? The people at Clarke's know the history of the instrument. In a real sense, they *are* the history of the instrument. Musician, Musicologist, and Educator Norman Dannatt is almost insufferably smart and knowledgeable and, in him, we have a marriage of scholarship, wit, and just plain fun brought to bear in this wonderful little volume. Enjoy the book and enjoy your whistle!

Dale Wisely
Chiff & Fipple: The Poststructural Tinwhistle Internet Experience

Introduction

*I*n the year 1843 Dickens published *A Christmas Carol*, Mendelssohn wrote his famous *Wedding March*, Wagner's opera *The Flying Dutchman* had its first performance, Brunel's tunnel under the Thames from Wapping to Rotherhithe was opened, John Curwen published his *Tonic Solfa*, Nelson's Column was erected in Trafalgar Square...

...and in a tiny, far from famous, village in Suffolk, Robert Clarke made his first Pennywhistle.

In 1843, in Coney Weston, that tiny village in Suffolk, a farm labourer made a small miracle. This was Robert Clarke, uneducated, hard-working, deeply religious and devoted to his family. He was also very musical. So much so, that he made his own musical instrument. This was the Tinwhistle. What was so miraculous was that his Tinwhistle produced a unique sound, on which, though attempts have been made to copy it, no one has ever improved.

Thanks to Robert's manufacturing and entrepreneurial skills, his instruments were later to be exported all over the globe.

The Clarke Tinwhistle has been the favourite instrument of many distinguished tinwhistle players ever since.

To celebrate the 150th Anniversary of the introduction of Robert Clarke's modest yet beautiful little invention to the history of music, I was asked to research the story of

Robert's Tinwhistle and family.

I offer this small volume for the interest of, not only those who are interested in the Tinwhistle and its incredibly large and varied world-wide repertoire, but also to anyone else who simply enjoys a good success story.

Norman Dannatt – May 1993

Introduction to Second Edition

Since I wrote the First Edition many people, including members of the Clarke Family, have contacted me and given me further information. The First Edition is now long sold out and all these new items of information have encouraged me to produce a Second Edition. It has also given me the chance to correct earlier mistakes, such as making the earliest Magdelenian flute 162,000 years older than it is.

Norman Dannatt – February 2005

Robert Clarke and his family

Life was extremely hard in East Anglia for farmers and their labourers during part of the first half of the 19th Century.

A series of disastrous wet seasons had ruined the crops and brought many farmers to bankruptcy. Very few survived. In fact, only one farmer brought his farm successfully through this period. He had invented a system of drainage that enabled him to cope with the constant inundation. He gradually bought up the lands of the other farmers who had failed and became rich and prosperous.

Many of the workers left Suffolk at this time and went either to Lancashire or emigrated to Australia or America.

During this period, a farm labourer by the name of Robert Clarke was determined that he and his family would not suffer if he could help it.

In a note book hand-written after Robert's death by James Clarke, his grandson, is a description of him:

> Mr Clarke was born in Coney Weston, a country village in the county of Suffolk, from very humble parents. His mother was a very pious hard working, God fearing woman. He was always known as a quiet inoffensive youth, never an angry word for anyone, but a pleasant look and smile for all he met, or was in company with. He was a farmer's labourer in

1. Coney Weston Church

early life, therefore not having very high wages, only from 7 shillings to 9 shillings per week. He was very industrious, his leisure hours devoted to music and a constant player on Sundays in the two Parish churches, Coney Weston (Picture 1) and Barningham, both farming districts.

His intentions were always good and honest trying to improve himself and save money from the fact that before he was married had saved over twenty pounds from his small earnings of 7/-per week.

He began to have an idea of travelling and selling whistles, which he was very determined on as he was confident of success – and instead of lying down in the fields after eating his dinner he was to be found in a corner of the field scraping and filing away at a piece of steel to make punches with and a saw from an old piece of steel from stays which were formerly worn by women, not having any spare money to buy proper material with, but would make any kind of thing do, that he might make a start of his business – his fellow workmen making fun and ridiculing, not knowing what he had in view, but he still persevered, prospered and accomplished what he intended.

George Goddard, presumably related to the Clarkes (Robert's wife was Sarah Goddard), wrote an article in the *Oldham Chronicle* in October 1953 describing Robert's activities:

> …He also had a flair for inventing things. One of his conceptions eventually developed into the making of the first Pennywhistle as we know it today… He gave a few of these whistles to his friends who were delighted with them. He could not afford to give them all away, so he made a small charge for them. It was not long before the village resounded to "God save the Queen", "Rule Britannia", Suffolk folk songs and hymns. People from neighbouring parishes came to see and hear this wonderful instrument, and wondered whether Robert could do anything for them.
>
> All these unusual activities got to the ears of the farmers, the parson and squire, and they were not too pleased with it. It disturbed the serenity of the countryside.
>
> Robert continued with his farm work and made whistles in what spare time he had and life became more tolerable with the little extra he earned.
>
> Then came a bombshell. One Saturday afternoon, when Robert went to collect his wages, instead of receiving 9s he only received 8s 11d. Thinking a mistake had been made he drew the attention of the farmer to the missing penny. "It's all right," said the farmer, "Instead of takin' fifty loads o' manure on't fields tha' only took forty-nine, and that's why I've stopped t' penny." Robert strongly denied this and said he had taken all to the fields, as was the usual custom. However, the farmer refused to pay the penny. Robert thereupon told the farmer that it was not only the penny that mattered, it was the slight on his character, which he deeply resented.
>
> The farmer was still adamant. Then Robert told the farmer that if he did not pay the penny, he would chuck up his job. Somewhat surprised the farmer said, "An' where wilt go?" It was most unusual for a farm worker to talk to his employer like this.
>
> The news flashed round the countryside and there was general sympathy for Robert. When he went home and told his wife, it was sad news, but she had great faith in him.

Strangely enough, there came into Robert's hands a newspaper and among items of news was one to the effect that trade was fairly busy in Lancashire. After consulting with his wife, he decided that he would go to Lancashire, and, for the time being, would leave his wife and family in Suffolk.

The great great granddaughter of Robert Clarke, Janice Clarke, told me that Robert, on leaving the farm, used to walk for some time to Lowestoft, bought fish off the boats there, sold it on the way back to Coney Weston, gradually saving up enough money with which to make the journey. In fact, in the 1851 census, he was registered as a hawker, and he may have given himself that appellation following his time as a fish salesman.

He visited a friendly blacksmith who made him some simple tools with which he could make tinwhistles in greater quantity and taught him, as he would an apprentice, the techniques of metalwork.

I visited Harry Tomlinson, the widower of Doris (née Clarke), the great granddaughter of Robert, who gave me further information about how Robert came to design his whistles. Apparently he owned a wooden whistle (Harry says it was bamboo) which was conical in shape. This he copied in tinplate and thereafter all his whistles kept the conical shape.

He loaded Tinwhistles, materials, tools and his personal needs onto a handcart and, together with his son, set off on foot to walk to Manchester. (Picture 2) The difficulties and deprivations such a journey would afford can only be imagined. They would probably have either slept rough in the fields, or perhaps more comfortably in barns of friendly farmers. Harry Tomlinson told me that Robert's usual practice was to set up his handcart as a portable workshop in marketplaces. When interested people had gathered round to watch the Tinwhistle being made, he would play the music of the day as part of his sales pitch. His masterpiece was the *Londonderry Air*. He then offered his wares for sale. He made two sizes of whistle for sale – a large one and a small one. He was not beyond stopping to play the Tinwhistle to entertain people he met on the way and might even have picked up the odd penny or two for doing so. To recompense hospitable farmers Robert gave their children Tinwhistles as presents.

George Goddard tells that he would play for Irish labourers on the farms, extending his repertoire to *Come back to Erin*, *The harp that once through Tara's halls* and the songs of Tom Moore, the Irish poet.

Robert eventually arrived in Manchester, tired but determined. He took a hut in the vicinity of London Road Station and there he started to make his Tinwhistles and Manchester made him welcome. The public bought all the Tinwhistles he could make. James Clarke wrote:

> ◆ He ... continued for many years undergoing great hardships, not being able to get home very often to his wife and family, which he dearly loved – no man on earth was more attached to his home and children than he and which would feel very sweet indeed after being away from 6 to 12 months at a time. On one occasion at his return home he was paying

2. Robert Clarke and his son walking to Manchester

a visit to his Father-in-law, who lived close by. The squire's good lady called in almost at the same time being a constant visitor of his Father-in-law's, but was so overjoyed at seeing him home once more that she was forced to leave the room and weep – but soon returned to shake hands and welcome him home to his wife and children.

There is no mention as to how his wife and children managed at the time. Robert's work on the farm would most likely have brought with it a tied cottage, which he would have forfeited when he left. Perhaps the family stayed with relatives, of which there were many in that district. It could be that he might have given his wife the twenty pounds he had saved with which she might have rented accommodation for the time being. Maybe the Squire's good lady, being such a friend, might have helped. It is known she lived in the nearby village of Barningham. Robert would certainly have sent money home to his wife from what he earned by making and selling his Tinwhistles. The 1851 census shows Robert's in-laws living at Hal Farm House (presumably as tenants – possibly a tied cottage of the Squire's).

George Goddard wrote:

> Being a man of the country, however, he longed for more fresh air. One dinner hour, he was strolling down Market Street when he saw cattle being driven from Salford Cattle market.
>
> Robert liked the look of them and decided there and then that wherever those cattle went he would make his home. So he followed them with the drover. Their destination was Wynne's Farm, New Moston, (now demolished, the building stood on the site of the present recreation ground.) He took a house on Jones Street (now Eastwood Road). It had a building at the rear of the house and here he made his home and his whistles. Being established he went to Suffolk and brought back his wife and family…

James Clarke gives a different account of how the family came to join Robert:

> Soon after this he took a house in Manchester, being almost his first attempt at the wholesale business, but unfortunately

3. The two cottages built by Robert Clarke, 13 & 15 Jones Street (now Eastwood Road)

fell down sick almost to death. He sent for Mrs Clarke to come and wait on him and soon his family was bought to Manchester to live and settle down which they did for about five years and saved money enough to build himself two cottage houses (Picture 3) – one to live in and the other as a workshop – he always had a strong desire from a boy to have a house of his own that he might live and not be molested by anyone, but would not attempt to build until he had sufficient money to pay for it cash down, as his motto was to have money in hand to pay for anything before he got it. He would never borrow money but would go without that which he could not pay for and times without number he would exclaim how the Lord prospered him and that we ought not to forget how good the Lord was to him and all his family.

The family's arrival in Manchester was some time between 1850 and 1858; and they moved to New Moston in 1862 or 1863.

George Goddard says that Robert sent to Suffolk for his relatives, Mr. and Mrs. Goddard with their two youngest children, Henry and Ellen. Their two other sons, John and James, came later. Together with the Goddards the business expanded. Soon Clarke's Tinwhistles had a national reputation, even extending to the Continent. Local boys were also employed half time and New Moston became a hive of industry.

In June 1861 the family moved to the two cottages he had built in Jones Street (the census was earlier so in that they appeared on Bailey Street.). No. 13 was a cottage that had a cellar. No. 15 was the workshop, which was used as a storage space and then used by Robert, the son, as a home. At some stage, the proper workshop was built (No. 15a) behind No. 15. Bryan Shaw who lives in New Moston sent me a picture of the workshop (Picture 4), which he drew, from his bedroom window, when he was a schoolboy. The 1861 census shows Robert and his son Robert, both registered as tin flute makers. Bernard Savage, The New Moston History Society's archivist, who lives not far from the site of the old whistle factory, tells me that Robert planted trees there, one for each of his children. They are still there but have had to be lopped as they've grown so huge.

The 1871 census shows the whole family, Robert and his wife Sarah (Picture 5), together with their children, Amelia, Honor, Frederick and James were living in Jones Street.

Of the last two children, Frederick was born in Manchester and James was born in New Moston. Robert was registered,

4.
The Tinwhistle factory, 15a Jones Street

not as a Tinwhistle manufacturer, but as a tinplate worker. He is also shown as employing 4 men and 8 boys, so the business must have been thriving. Also in the same census, his son Robert is shown as living in Jones Street with his wife Alice and family of five children. He also is registered as a tin-plate worker.

By 1865 another Goddard family had joined Robert in New Moston and were living in Jones Street.

These were Charles Goddard (Picture 6), his wife Ann and two children, Elizabeth and Emma. Strangely, Charles Goddard is registered in the 1871 census as a tinwhistle

5. Robert & Sarah Clarke

6. Charles Goddard

maker, not a tin-plate worker.

By 1888 the trade directory shows four Clarkes registered as tinwhistle manufacturers:

Robert, tinwhistle manufacturer, New Moston

Robert, tinwhistle manufacturer, Weston House, New Moston

Frederick, tinwhistle manufacturer, Ballure House, New Moston

James, tinwhistle manufacturer, New Moston

As Robert, the inventor of the Clarke Pennywhistle, died on the 24th of August 1892, the two Roberts mentioned are his son, known as "Robert-the-son" and his son, known as "Young Robert".

The 1861 census shows Amelia Clarke, the daughter of the first Robert, registered as a tin flute maker. She was then 13 years of age.

Robert-the-son and James continued making Tinwhistles, although the 1891 registry shows them as 'Tinwhistle and Cycle makers', and then in 1895 back as tinwhistle makers exclusively.

Both Frederick and James were enthusiastic cyclists. Frederick became one of the first North of England cycling champions. (Picture 7) As well as racing, he used to tour the country on his bicycle. He soldered a gold sovereign onto the frame of his bicycle, which he said would act as an insurance against financial difficulties on the road. By 1910 Frederick seemed to have given up Tinwhistle work and was now registered in the trade registry as a cycle and motor manufacturer and later, in 1925, as a motor manufacturer. Harry Tomlinson told me that the sons, Frederick, James and Robert, did try to carry on the Tinwhistle manufacture but, unlike their father, they had been brought up in the lap of luxury and though they were clever workmen, they had no idea of business and, when the First World War came, they were ordered to do war work.

In 1910 the brothers engineered the first motorcycle. Bernard Savage told me about this machine. It was a converted bicycle, with a small engine in the back wheel. (It was years ahead of its time. This idea surfaced again just after

7. Frederick Clarke

the 1939-45 War as the "Cyclemaster".) It had a carburettor made out of a Tate and Lyle treacle tin! The little engine had two cylinders and was cranked directly onto the spindle of the back wheel. The only way they could give the machine a road test was to do it at 5 a.m. and they had to bribe the local Bobby five shilling to look the other way. Unfortunately the power stroke was too strong, making the wheel accelerate far too powerfully and consequently the tyre was worn out in less than seven miles. Frederick presented his motorcycle to the Science Museum; then later, unexpectedly, withdrew it. The machine lay in his shed thereafter until it rotted away. I tried to find out something about it in the museum but the curator had absolutely no record of its ever having been there.

Frederick and his son, Frederick James, actually built a motor car from scratch. Frederick worked for some time as chief assistant to a man called Royce, manufacturing early cars. Royce felt that there were better engineering opportunities in Derby than in Manchester and asked Frederick to go there with him. Foolishly Frederick refused to go and must have regretted it ever since, because Royce had become involved with another man called Rolls and the rest is, as they say, history!

Robert was a deeply religious man. He always maintained that his prosperity as inventor and manufacturer of the Tinwhistle was the Lord's work. Together with a friend named George Barton he formed a group of Primitive Methodists in a house called the "Gilded Hollies".

George Barton was a fine musician and he and Robert formed a small orchestra that played for the services. Eventually the congregation became too large for the "Gilded Hollies" and in 1881 a new chapel was opened in Jones Street, financed largely by Robert. (Picture 8)

8. Robert's Primitive Methodist Chapel in Eastwood Road, c.1901

An interesting aspect of Robert's character was that he deeply distrusted banks and similar financial institutions. He kept his not inconsiderable fortune, in gold sovereigns, in buckets in his cellar!

It is said in the hand-written notebook that Robert's death was a happy one. He had suffered from a sickness of a "lingering kind". His doctor had called for the help of a specialist. Robert-the-son was standing by the window and he saw the train arriving with a specialist on board. He told his father, who answered, "My train won't be long. I am ready waiting, which is only a short time." On the next day, he tried to put his hands together to pray, but was not strong enough. Members of his family who were with him helped him clasp his hands and he whispered his last words, "Lord Jesus", or, "Lord have mercy". His death was like a child's, his breathing so gentle and easy. He passed away as in an easy sleep. (Picture 9)

9. The gravestones of Robert Clarke and Charles Goddard

The family continued to make the Tinwhistles and by 1902, under the proprietorship of James Clarke, Tinwhistles with a wide range of keys were in the firm's catalogue. (Picture 10)

They even made pea-shooters and cycle whistles. Apparently in the days of the penny-farthing bicycle, there were cycle clubs with membership of anything up to 200 members. They wore elaborate uniforms covered with gold braid. Mounting, setting off, stopping and dismounting was all done with military precision, with the leader's blowing, originally, a bugle. A cycle whistle later replaced the bugle. Robert's sons were members of a cycle club and it was only natural that Robert would have made whistles for them and later, commercially, for the whole cycling fraternity. I have seen many cycle whistles in museums, but up to the present have not found a single Clarke cycle whistle. The cycle whistles that are in the Lincoln Cycle Museum are elaborate ones made of silver. Perhaps the clubs became so important and influential that mere tin cycle whistles would have been considered infra dig. We are still searching for a Clarke pea-shooter. I owned one as a boy, but such a toy would have had a limited life and possibly none have survived. Mine didn't!

The instruments were widely exported abroad, mostly under the Clarke name, although one dealer in Germany sold them under his own name. In that case the Tinwhistles were sent to him with the "R. Clarke" logo scratched off

10. The 1903 Lyon and Healy price list showing Clarke Tinwhistles

11. The Clarke "Fluit" as sold in Holland

12. Front cover of a Fresco brochure showing how Clarke gave permission for Fresco to change the name of the Tinwhistle from Clarke to his own name and the Exhibition medallions presumably won by Fresco for 'his' whistles

and he replaced it with his own logo – "A.Fresco". (Picture 12) In Holland the Clarke "Fluit" was "wereldberoemd" (world famous). (Picture 11)

An American firm, C. Bruno and Son, included the Tinwhistles among other makes in their catalogue, although there seems to be some doubt about the correct names of the instruments. (Picture 13) It is interesting to note that today, C.Bruno and Son (now a subsidiary of the Kaman Corporation) continues to sell

Clarke Tinwhistles. One of the Tinwhistles pictured could be the so-called "Crystallised Whistle" but it is called a "fife". The other, with the logo G. CLARK'S LONDON MAKE, looks like a Robert Clarke Tinwhistle. Perhaps Bruno renamed the Tinwhistles hoping that the London cachet might make it a better seller or maybe there was a G. Clarke in London making whistles under licence from Robert. We know that a nephew of Robert's, Charles Clarke, together with his son Daniel, made the instruments in Hackney but we do not know under what name they marketed them. The spelling of names in early days was rather haphazard. Many people were illiterate and would rely on others to write their names down, often with doubtful spelling. Robert Clarke himself was illiterate. Both he and his wife signed their names with X's on their marriage lines in the Church records.

James Clarke's factory remained at 13a Eastwood Road. There were several fireplaces in the factory, not all for warmth. One, a coke fire, was in continual use for heating the soldering irons. Another was used to melt the big lumps of lead solder in ladles. The lead was then poured into triangular shaped moulds to make convenient sticks for use. Alan Clarke described to me how James used to make his own flux in the yard. This was a highly dangerous process and needed the open air for safety's sake. This process involved pouring hydrochloric acid explosively on lime chippings in a big vat.

13. A page from the 1900 C. Bruno & Son catalogue

When James died in 1943 the manufacture of Tinwhistles stopped for a while and the factory was let to a Mr Croft who, with a partner, started a car body repairs firm. At some stage, when body repairing was slack, these two men started making the Tinwhistles for a time.

Frederick Stanley Clarke (Picture 16) and his brother Eric started making the Tinwhistles soon after the 1939-45 War in another building. The houses in Eastwood Road had been knocked down after a compulsory order. Business was very brisk. One order, for example, from a South African shipper, was for one ton of Clarke Tinwhistles, painted red, for the Belgian Congo! I wonder if somewhere in a village in Congo, a red painted whistle is still being played.

These pictures were taken in 1986 shortly before the move to Tonbridge (Picture 14 and 15).

14. The last Tinwhistle factory in New Moston

15. Inside the old factory

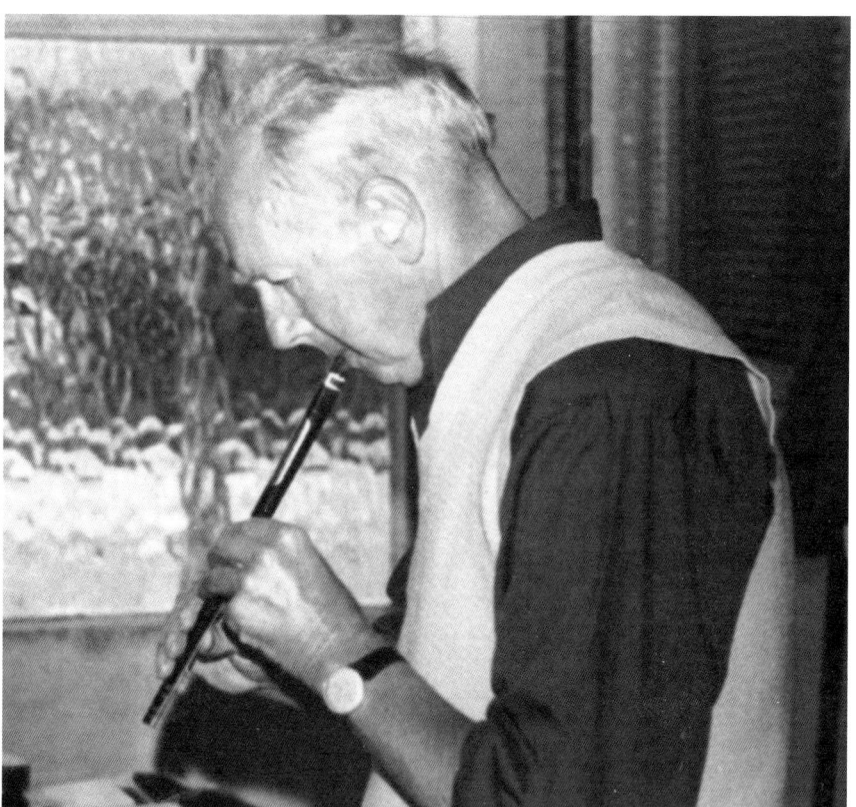

16. Fred Clarke in the last New Moston factory

Anne Howard, the daughter of Eric Clarke, describes how her father and Fred restarted production after the war. It was not possible at that time to have the sheets of tin plate printed with the black colour so the brothers made the Tinwhistles in natural tin plate and then dipped them in whatever paint they were able to obtain. The colours of these Tinwhistles were red, yellow, green or blue.

When I visited Harry Tomlinson, he told me that his grandfather's brother's daughter was a missionary in Northern Rhodesia. She was Elsie Wyman, MBE. As she ran a school, Harry obtained and sent her 3 gross (432) of Clarke's Tinwhistles. They were meant for the children to play in the school. The parents of the children took the whistles away from them and kept them for themselves.

Such an instrument would have been a great treasure to those very poor and primitive people – not to be wasted on schoolchildren. Again, I wonder if any of those whistles still exist in the villages in Zambia.

The manufacture of the Tinwhistles remained with the family until 1986 and the last managing director was Fred Clarke. Together with his wife Lily, his sister-in-law Mary and niece Joan, he kept up a stream of Tinwhistles, but barely kept pace with the orders that flooded in. He tested his whistles on completion by blowing them on the back end of an old vacuum cleaner.

Fred was heard to say, "We just don't tell anyone just how we make the whistles, and our production figures are secret too. We're a happy family firm. We can't keep up with the demand for our products, but we don't want to get bigger. It would only mean getting bogged down with a lot of book-keeping and extra paper work."

The Weedons

In the summer of 1964, a young man called Jim Weedon spent his holidays in Norfolk, England. Earlier that year Jim had joined a London musical instrument wholesaler as a clerk. During this vacation he met a young woman called Carol Jones, also on vacation, and fell completely under her spell. At that time it is scarcely surprising that nothing was further from his mind than a small Tinwhistle company founded just across the county border in Coney Weston, Suffolk, 100 years before his birth. Coincidently Jim was born only a few miles from Coney Weston, in the historic town of Bury St. Edmunds, Suffolk. Omens, perhaps! Carol obviously saw something in Jim too, for they rapidly became friends and married in 1966, having determined to spend the rest of their lives together.

Jim continued his career with the wholesale company, rising through the ranks as Sales Manager, Director, then Managing Director. One of the many lines he distributed in that capacity was the Clarke Tinwhistle and during this time he came into contact with the company's last Managing Director, Frederick Stanley Clarke. Mr Clarke eventually decided to sell the business as presumably neither of his children, Stanley and Joan, wished to carry it on. So it was that in 1986 the business came up for sale and there were a number of potential buyers. Who but Jim

17. The New Owners – Carol & Jim Weedon

Weedon would turn out to be the successful purchaser, with his many years of experience in the music industry behind him? Jim paid for the business with a lump sum and then came a charming, poetical touch. For the next five years, Jim subsequently paid Fred one penny for each Tinwhistle he made and sold!

Knowing that this venture needed family hands-on attention, Jim and Carol committed themselves to securing the future of the Clarke Tinwhistle. (Picture 17) They rented a space in the warehouse of the wholesale company that Jim worked for (then in Tonbridge, Kent) and moved the contents of the New Moston Tinwhistle factory there. It took up one small room! Fred Clarke's old building became a factory for photographic chemicals. Before the move Jim had asked Brian Woolf, a colleague and part-time music teacher, to spend some time in the old factory working with Fred Clarke, to absorb the old manufacturing techniques. With the knowledge acquired Jim and Carol began to work in their own time making

Clarke Tinwhistles. The machinery was old and nearly worn out and needed replacing. Carol spent much of her time working with some of the pieces of the original machinery at home, in their bedroom, making Tinwhistles to sell, creating the income needed for research and development. Then, finally, the whole process of manufacture was moved to the Tonbridge warehouse.

Jim has always been meticulously careful in everything that he does. He was determined that his new enterprise would start off in the right direction and to this end he enlisted the help of Bill Ochs (see Page 81), the celebrated American tinwhistler and authority on Irish music. Jim sent a batch of his newly-made Tinwhistles to Bill and asked him to give advice on how to get the optimum tone and accuracy of tuning. Bill worked hard on them, finely adjusting the metal in the mouthpiece (affectionately known as "tweaking"), so that he came up with the definitive tuning and toning of the whistles. The methods he used were much the same as organ tuners use on the fipple pipes of the organs. Jim adopted Bill's improvements when his little factory went into full production. New equipment was developed on the same lines as the original, but using modern technology. However, although improvements were built into the new machinery, the basic manufacturing principles have always remained the same.

In May 1993, Jim, feeling that the business needed and could support his full-time attention, took the plunge by leaving his employment of nearly 30 years. The family nature of the business is as strong today as ever it was with the Clarkes. In addition to Jim and Carol, their sons, Michael (business administrator for the firm) and Paul (in sales and promotion) worked together in the production of Tinwhistles. Their youngest son, James, did not enter the business but has followed an early ambition by becoming a printer.

Sadly, after a long illness, Carol died leaving Jim heartbroken. The Tunbridge Wells Crematorium was full of mourners, friends and staff members of Jim's previous company and the Clarke company. As Carol was borne into the chapel, Goretti Anglim, (Picture 38) the Irish whistler, played an air on her Tinwhistle – "Do not wake me, I am only sleeping" – a tune traditionally played at Irish interments. After it is played the whistle is laid on the coffin and is buried with it. In this case, Goretti handed her Tinwhistle to Jim, who placed it in a display cabinet, never to be played again.

Jim recognised the importance of the historical background and it was decided that Brian Woolf should go to Coney Weston and find out what he could of the history of Clarke Tinwhistles. He visited the village and made enquiries there. He also photographed several of the buildings that were in the village when Robert Clarke lived there. He was given copies of the parish magazine and found the following article by Julian Flood, who lives in Coney Weston:

> ◆ Coney Weston never fails to amaze me. A couple of weeks ago I saw a man wandering around the street with a camera, looking lost, so, being of a kindly and nosy disposition I went along to help. He was the production manager of a small Pennywhistle firm – no, really, I'm not pulling your leg, he really was. Some years ago his company brought out a small firm in Manchester which made a rather nice and unusual Pennywhistle, tapered in the barrel and with a wooden insert in the mouthpiece. He showed me one, and I managed to get a tune out of it, and I remembered seeing a picture of one in a Clancy Brothers' book, so he wasn't pulling my leg either. He had been to Manchester to get the machinery and move it to Kent, and had talked to the seller who was a descendant of the original owner...
>
> ...Mr Woolf discovered that the founder of the firm had started out in Coney Weston. In 1843 he had been short of work as a farm labourer, as it was a poor summer, so he got his friend in the forge to make him some tools, and he passed the year making and selling Pennywhistles. Then he thought he would seek his fortune, so he loaded the tools on a handcart and walked to Manchester.
>
> His name was Robert Clarke and as you still can't throw a clematis a yard in Coney Weston without hitting a Clarke,

one wonders if he is related to the families still living in this area. He was born in 1816, and that is all I know. How can I trace him, or the forge in 1843? Which farm did he work for? Help from anyone with experience in this sort of detective work would be appreciated.

Next time you are in New York nip into a music shop and ask for a Clarke Pennywhistle. On the back of the pack you'll find the history of the firm, and the name of Coney Weston. Fame indeed!

Julian Flood is himself a Tinwhistle player. He is rather proud that while in the RAF in Canada, he played "The Campdown Races" on his Tinwhistle while flying a Buccaneer from 120 to 150 feet at 530 to 550 knots! He says he has the record for high speed, low flying, Tinwhistle playing. I wonder how his navigator's nerves suffered!

Margery Hammond who lives in Barningham, a nearby village, saw Julian Flood's article and answered in a subsequent magazine:

> I was very interested to read Julian Flood's article about the tinwhistle man. I cannot remember having heard this name before, and have no idea where he lived or worked in his youth, but I know that the last years of his life were spent at Market Weston. My late father often told of an experience which his father had, and which I think must have been in the 1880's or 1890's. I pass it on now. My grandfather, Charles Hammond, lived at the Garden House at Weston Market, and was a market gardener, taking his produce to Thetford weekly with a horse and cart. He always stabled his horse at a certain public house, and one day when he went in to take some refreshments before his journey home, the landlord introduced to him an elderly man, who said he wanted to go to Market Weston, and he asked my grandfather if he would be leaving. The traveller was a rough-looking man, carrying an old bag like a workman's tool bag. He said he had just one more piece of business to attend to in Thetford, and asked if he could leave his bag with my grandfather, as it was rather heavy to carry around with him. At the stated time he returned, and they set off for Market Weston.

On the way, they talked together, and my grandfather found that the stranger seemed to know the district quite well, and was enquiring about various people and places. As they got near to Market Weston, the old man told my grandfather that he had come to buy a certain property in the village. Grandfather was somewhat taken aback, as he looked little better than a tramp. He obviously guessed what my grandfather was thinking, for he said, "You think I haven't the money to buy that place. You little thought that the bag I asked you to look after was full of gold sovereigns. I had asked the landlord about you and he said you were an honest man, so I knew it would be safe with you." He showed my grandfather the money, telling him that he had made his fortune by the manufacture of tinwhistles. Before they parted, he took a whistle from his pocket and played a tune for my grandfather, who said that he had never heard a tinwhistle played so beautifully.

The place the old man bought was a little property next to Fen Farm at Market Weston. In the early years of this century, my grandfather took over the tenancy of Fen Farm, and my father used to recall that when they were living there, the neighbouring property was still known as Tinwhistle Farm, although by that time the old man was dead and it had other owners. I hope this will be of interest to Julian Flood and other readers. Is the name "Tinwhistle Farm" still in use, I wonder? Or has the property long since been absorbed into Fen Farm?

Julian Flood has written the following footnote to the above article:

> They have long memories in Suffolk!

Presumably the bag of gold sovereigns which Robert carried was part of the hoard in the buckets in the cellar of his house.

As well as the research in Coney Weston, information has also been sought about other types of Clarke whistles. Frederick Clarke confirmed that the original instruments that Robert made were called "Megs", the Lancashire name for a halfpenny. This word has for all intents and purposes

18. The Crystallised Whistle

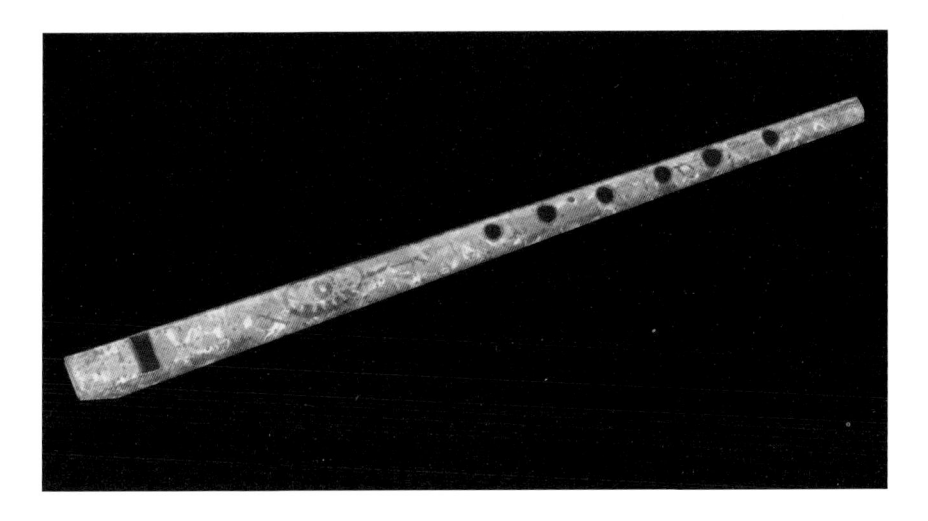

almost disappeared from the language. It appears in a poem by Leslie Jowett:-

"Wi'd spendin' brass just once a week that bowt us bits a stuff,
But two megs each didn't go far, wi thowt not awf enuff,
It sometimes bowt a cap bomb, tin whistle or tatie gun,
Or a basset juice an' kali lick wer allus lots a' fun."

The "Meg" was only a small size and it would be in a high pitch. Frederick sent Brian a blank but he felt that, although it was small, it was not a "Meg" as there was one even smaller. It is hoped that one can be found. Perhaps one day one will appear in a museum or a collection. We hope so. Recently a descendant of Robert Clarke, Alan Clarke, showed me a small brass whistle made by Robert. It is approximately in the key of A of our modern pitch. Whether or not it is a "Meg" we do not know. A unique Tinwhistle made by the Clarke's especially for the great exhibition in the Crystal Palace has been found. It has a mottled gold finish, and was known as a "Crystallised Whistle". (Picture 18)

There is a great mystery attached to the considerable list of Tinwhistles in a variety of keys that the firm was making and advertising. (Pictures 10 and 13) None of the family alive today has any information about them, either as to

19. The Clarke Team, 1993

size or manufacturing techniques. There are no patterns extant. Alan Clarke has more recently found several old Clarke whistles, made of brass in various keys, stored away in a corner of his house, but they are all in an early concert pitch. The Folk World is longing for the resurrection, for example, of the small Clarke Tinwhistle in G and, since the enormous success of *Riverdance*, whistle enthusiasts are crying out for a low Clarke Tinwhistle in D. Both of these will be projects for the firm to consider in the near future.

The Making of a Clarke Tinwhistle

asically the Clarke Tinwhistle consists of a sheet of tinplate, a piece of wood and a small quantity of solder; with or without black paint and gold lacquer.

But that, of course, is not the whole story. Somehow the young farm worker, Robert Clarke, put together these ingredients and produced a small artistic miracle.

The Tinwhistle buffs who know and prefer the original Clarke Tinwhistle, point to an indefinable quality which this whistle has. It is something to do with the tone. They call it "chiff". No other tinwhistle has quite the same degree of "chiff". The tone of the instrument is clear and flutelike, but it has an additional quality, a breathiness, even roughness, unique to itself and immediately recognisable to the listener. This is "chiff".

This basic type of whistle flute has a long history going back into the far distant past, even to prehistoric times. Bone flutes have been found from the Magdelanian Period – as long ago as 18,000 years. In more recent years it appeared as the flageolet and the recorder. When tin plate was easy to get and not expensive, early in the Industrial Revolution in England, the way was open for Robert Clarke to make a whistle from that material. Previously the recorder and flageolet were made from wood and other natural materials. The one characteristic, which all these instruments shared, was called the fipple. This was simply a plug, usually of wood, pushed into the mouthpiece, with a narrow gap between it and the wall of the mouthpiece through which the wind is blown. Below it is the window, an opening with a wedge-shaped lower part that directs and forms the wind column to produce the sound. This sound is then controlled by holes further down the pipe which are covered or opened by the fingers. The recorder has a thumbhole at the back and seven basic holes on the front of the instrument, although in more recent times the bottom two holes are often divided into two holes each to provide the lowest half notes. The flageolet had six holes, two of which were at the back and controlled by the thumbs. The Tinwhistle has six holes, all in front. In manufacture, the size and shape of the wind channel between the fipple and the wall of the Tinwhistle is carefully adjusted to get the correct tone and degree of chiff. Players all have their own preferences and adjust this gap to suit these preferences. I have watched an old street tinwhistler called Jock MacLean altering his Clarke Tinwhistle from time to time with a nail file which, he assures listeners, is an authentic tuning key! Christoph Heyl of the Johann Wolfgang Goethe University in Frankfurt tells us that he is an enthusiastic player of Clarke Tinwhistles, not only for their superior performance but also that it is possible to make minute adjustments to the mouthpiece. He says that using simple techniques such as those usually employed by organ builders, it is possible to make individual instruments ideal for quiet, precise solo performance or to give them a more powerful ensemble voice. At some time a pamphlet was issued by Bill Ochs giving instructions to players as to how to adjust the whistles to suit their own taste. We would not recommend everyone to attempt this unless they really know what they are doing.

One of the tools which the blacksmith in Suffolk must have made for Robert Clarke was a conical mandrel. Round this Robert rolled the tinplate which he had already cut to shape and holed for the finger holes and window. Then he soldered down the length of the joint. He would have already shaped the fipple with his saw made out of the piece of steel from a lady's stays. He pushed the fipple into the mouthpiece and fixed it there by simply tapping small punch holes through the metal to the wood. Then he would have voiced the instrument by blowing and adjusting the shape of the wind channel over and below the fipple. He was very musical and would have made sure that the instrument was properly in tune and had the correct tonal qualities. The metal was then either left plain or lacquered.

As time went on and the factory prospered, Robert introduced simple machinery into the manufacture. There was a mechanical punch that would have cut all the holes in one movement. The black lacquer with its characteristic golden Clarke logo was eventually printed on the tin plate before cutting the shape out. The soldering burnt the paint-work all along the back of the instrument, so that it had to be cleaned up and fresh paint applied with a brush. Ann Howard, the daughter of Eric Clarke, remembers how her father and his brother Fred used to single-colour dip the whistles when production was resumed after the 1939-45 War. These whistles were red, yellow and either blue or green. They were just plain whistles dipped into paint because it was not possible to have the sheets of tinplate printed. Later the black and gold lacquer printing was introduced.

Another living member of the Clarke family, Alan Clarke, describes how he remembers watching his grandfather, (James Snr., Robert's youngest son), making the whistles in the workshop on Eastwood Road (known as Jones Street pre 1905). He said there was no electricity. Power came from a gas engine and 3 inch leather belts 'took the power' to the lathes and drills etc.

When Fred Clarke sold the business to Jim Weedon, the machinery proved to be almost worn out, but manufacture continued and increased. Gradually the machinery was rebuilt or replaced and improved techniques of manufacture were introduced. The characteristic black and gold livery was once more printed on the tinplate before cutting and soldering.

Considerable research was put into use of materials and the speeding up of the work. Several different materials were tried out to improve the fipples – plastics, resin-bonded materials, metal. Continual playing of a Clarke Tinwhistle tended to make the fipple go soggy and affect the tone, hence the search for something better. Unfortunately all the materials tried reduced the tonal quality of the instrument with deterioration of the chiff. Eventually, Jim was forced to come back to wood again. The only difference was that the more expensive, and harder, cedar or maple wood now replaced the original Malayan rubber-tree wood used by Clarke. Being very resinous, it is not as absorbent as Clarke's original wood, but it preserves the tonal quality. The wood has to be such that it comes out very smooth when cut across the grain. The disastrous gales in 1987 destroyed vast acres of woodland in the south of England and, suddenly, valuable cedar wood became readily available from the fallen trees. An ill wind certainly blew Clarkes good! Over the years, players have resorted to their own methods of preserving the wood – waxing it or coating it with a wood sealant. Ciaran Carsen in his *Guide to Traditional Irish music* (1986) tells how Jim Donoghue, the Sligo whistle player, doctored the wood with a heated hacksaw blade, which seems to have given the whistle a very loud trumpet-like tone.

The method of painting the instrument was still continued, together with the time-consuming repainting of the joint after the soldering. Many methods were tried to overcome this problem and eventually it was decided to solder the unpainted instruments and then to apply a dry resin paint that was later melted onto the metal in an oven. A slightly different design of the livery painting has had to be made to accommodate the new dry technique and the logo has been redesigned.

Otherwise, at a first glance, it is still the same instrument and it definitely still sounds the same – chiff and all!

The Tinwhistle had acquired another name – "Pennywhistle". It was called Tinwhistle because it is made of tin-plated steel. The name Pennywhistle appeared sometime in the later part of the 1800s. However, it did not cost a penny – at least not at first, as already mentioned, when it was originally called a "Meg" – a halfpenny. Perhaps, as time went on, inflation put the price up to one penny. Certainly today the price is anything but one penny! It is said that the name "Pennywhistle" was derived from the fact that, in Victorian times, street musicians and urchins used to play it for pennies, but this is apocryphal. As time went on other makers of whistles called them Pennywhistles but that is quite wrong. The names "Tinwhistle" and "Pennywhistle" apply essentially and historically to Clarke's. One publisher, who had printed a whistle tutor book for children, sent a

20. Bill Ochs' packaging

Clarke Tinwhistle, actually a Sweetone (Picture 24), to a manufacturer in the Far East, and asked him to pirate it for inclusion in a bubble pack with the tutor book. As the book was smaller than a Sweetone, the publisher must have asked the manufacturer to shorten the whistle to make it fit the bubble pack. Cutting an inch off one end of the whistle and one and a half inches off the other end gave it the right length. The position of the finger holes remained the same. The resulting sound of the whistle was simply awful – all out of tune. Surprisingly the publisher went ahead and sold his tutor book with the whistle in the bubble pack. I saw them for sale in shops. Later I saw them for sale, greatly reduced in price, in cheap and cheerful shops. Jim keeps one of these bubble packs in his factory as a monstrous example of the sins of pirating our Tinwhistles.

The working staff of the new factory still remains quite small. The output increases to match the great demand from all over the world. This is the age of presentation and the Tinwhistles are now sold in elegant and attractive packaging with the story of the Clarke family printed on them. Bill Ochs' definitive Tutor & Cassette was also packaged together with the Clarke Tinwhistles. (Picture 20)

In 1991 a small industrial area in Five Oak Green, a village near Tonbridge, was re-developed. One of the buildings, known as the Old Joinery, had become vacant. (Picture 21) It was renovated and modernised, while still maintaining its earlier appearance of a small, oak beamed, workshop. Such a building immediately appealed to Jim Weedon as an eminently suitable place to manufacture the Pennywhistles. The machinery and equipment were moved from Tonbridge to Five Oak Green and installed in the Old Joinery, restoring the traditional appearance of the original cottage industry begun in a small building all those years ago by Robert Clarke. (Picture 4). In more recent years the Old Joinery became too small for the growing business and it has now been moved to larger premises immediately behind the Old Joinery. The address still remains the same, however.

Strangely, Five Oak Green and Coney Weston have

something in common in addition to the Tinwhistle. Coney Weston's church, St. Mary's, stands in fields more than a mile away from the village. The reason is that, during the Great Plague, the villagers who had not yet caught the disease relocated some distance from the village. In the course of time the remaining villagers died and their houses were allowed to decay. Now all that remains in that area is the church. Exactly the same thing happened in Five Oak Green. The village church, St. Thomas à Becket, also stands in fields some distance from what is now Five Oak Green.

An echo of those days occurred when the Tonbridge Joint Isolation Hospital for the treatment of infectious diseases was built in 1887 in Five Oak Green. Infected people from the surrounding district were brought there for treatment. Possibly the existence of healing springs in the village accounted for its choice as the location of the hospital. This hospital no longer exists.

Ever since folk musicians have played the Clarke Tinwhistle they have longed for a whistle in the key of D. The Tinwhistle which has always been available and which

21. The Old Joinery at Five Oak Green, Kent

22. Bob Bellingham

is still produced in great quantities is in the key of C. The main reason for the desired D Tinwhistle is that it plays more comfortably together with folk fiddles, which mostly tend to favour the keys of G and D. It is possible to play a C Tinwhistle in the key of D but it means starting the scale on the last but lowest hole and half covering certain other holes to get the sharp notes. As mentioned before, it is known that the early Robert Clarke firm made and catalogued a set of whistles in various keys. One of them, made of brass and approximately in the present day key of A is now in the possession of Alan Clarke. It is a beautiful little whistle with a very clear tone. Clarke's previous production manager, Bob Bellingham, (Picture 22) made a prototype copy of this little whistle in tin, but as he says, he had made it only for the pleasure of doing so, for the time being!

At last, however, Bob designed and developed the long awaited Tinwhistle in D. Sadly he died not long ago and is greatly missed; but the success of his new Tinwhistle stands as a memorial to him.

There has been great rejoicing in the Folk World over the arrival of that Tinwhistle in D, as can be seen from the following article by Tim Moon (Picture 47) which appeared in the Autumn 1989 copy of *Tykes' News*, a West Yorkshire Folk Magazine:

The Clarke's Whistle in D

The human world has many facets. There are things which are promised, but which never happen – like the concept album about The Tolpuddle Martyrs which Fairport were going to record. There are things which will just never happen, full stop. Like the human race turning round and saying what a rotten idea it is devoting so much time to shooting each other. There are things which have never been proved to exist, but on the other hand no one has ever proved that they don't, like the Loch Ness Monster. Drifting in and out of all these concepts was the Clarke's whistle in the key of D.*

It has been long promised and spent many years as a parental trick for unsuspecting offspring: "Daddy, can I have a new bike?" "You can have one as soon as the D whistle hits the shops, my daughter." But now the mythical beast itself (herein referred to as the CDW) has arrived... and all black with gold trim. Gosharootie! I've had the C version for years and love it dearly, despite fiddlers and squeezers playing in D and G. My Clarke's is scratched, has a little kink from being sat on, and the bit of wood in the mouthpiece looks like it could restart the Black Plague all by itself. And it sounds bloody great, all breathy and flute-like, and not so harsh as the more normal parallel bore whistles.

So the arrival of the CDW had me in paroxisms of joy; more joy than you can imagine available for the price. That smooth tone and that conical bore are there from the C and the size is, of course, a little less. The first thing you notice on playing is the ease of breath which means that you run out of breath in unexpected places, but it takes minutes to adjust and it's not a problem. Also it's a little more harsh than the C, though less so than its rivals, and I suspect it will soften as the wood gets a bit used to spit and swells a little. I've played it for some time since I bought it and

I can recommend this product with all my heart. And Clarke's haven't bribed me to say that, but I am not beyond being bribed by a Clarke's low G, if they'd care to produce one. Till then, this is like making love near to heaven. Now let's find the Loch Ness Monster. (© Tim-Life 1989)

*Tim Moon could not have been aware that the original firm did, in fact, make a D whistle (together with many other keys), but they went out of production many years ago.

For a long time Jim Weedon felt that there should be a Clarke Tinwhistle especially for children. One that was colourful, inexpensive and, if possible, childproof. The first consideration had to be the mouthpiece and the fipple. The traditional Clarke wooden fipple could be spoilt by playing immediately after eating sweets or burgers. The ideal mouthpiece had to be one made entirely of plastic. Considerable research went into designing the perfect plastic mouthpiece. I personally spent many happy hours gently filing a plastic prototype till I completely ruined it! To get the final touches of perfection to the design of the mouthpiece, Jim went all the way to the States and got the famous American instrument maker, Michael Copeland (Picture 23) to work on them. Michael achieved the perfect design and Jim took some of the new whistles to Bill Ochs for his approval. They were together in a Giftware trade show when Bill started to try out the whistles. A lady on a nearby stand objected to Bill's playing (she couldn't have been a music lover!) so Bill and Jim went outside to a loading bay where Bill tried out the whistles in peace. He declared them to be perfect – in fact good enough for professional players. It turned out later that his opinion was in every way correct.

The new Clarke whistle when completed was named the SWEETONE. (Picture 24) We thought that you can read this name whichever way you like – either "SWEET-ONE" or "SWEET-TONE". As it happens, it has been called "SWEET-TONE" ever since.

It is the first conical bore tinwhistle to have been made

with a plastic mouthpiece and available in a variety of bright cheerful colours. As we had hoped, it is easy to play; with a clear, accurate tone and readily affordable.

We felt that it would be the ideal instrument for the child or the beginner, leading naturally, later on, to the more advanced original Tinwhistle – the whistle for the professional player and the enthusiastic amateur.

Strangely enough however, it is those professional players and enthusiastic amateurs who are enjoying the Sweetone – not as an alternative to Clarke's Pennywhistle, but as an additional tinwhistle they can use for its contrasting tonal qualities – sweetness and delicacy as opposed to strength and robustness. The sound to match the mood of the tune being played.

The final accolade for the Sweetone, exceeding all our wildest ambitions, came when Dr. Dale Wisely (Picture 51) conducted a poll regarding visitors' favourite inexpensive whistles on his website on the Internet.

23. Michael Copeland

The Clarke Sweetone won handily!

Dale suggested that a version of the Sweetone should be manufactured, not brightly coloured – that's for the kids – but in natural, unpainted tinplate. A "Professional Model" in fact. Professional players are already sensitive to the concept held by many that the Tinwhistle is only a toy and they do not therefore appreciate the bright colours. Jim Weedon had already realised this so the instrument was made available in natural shiny tinplate. A truly "Professional Model". However, there is a problem. Some players have sweaty hands. The sweat can react with the tinplate causing it to go grey. For them an entirely black lacquered one has been made.

For some time Jim Weedon planned to produce another type of Sweetone specially for very little children. He wanted it to be a whistle of Fairyland. His team of ideasmen and artists got their heads together and came up with "The Enchanted Whistle". (Picture 25) It appeared green with a hint of brown creepers all over it. It was packaged together with a tutor book and a set of good quality coloured pencils. Instructions as to fingering the whistle are clearly laid out for each new note learnt, using a straightforward simplified musical notation. The tunes have words that describe, in an amusing way, some of the denizens of Fairyland. The children can play and then sing each song. There is a pretty picture of each member of Fairyland that can be coloured by the child after the relative tune has been played.

24. Sweetone

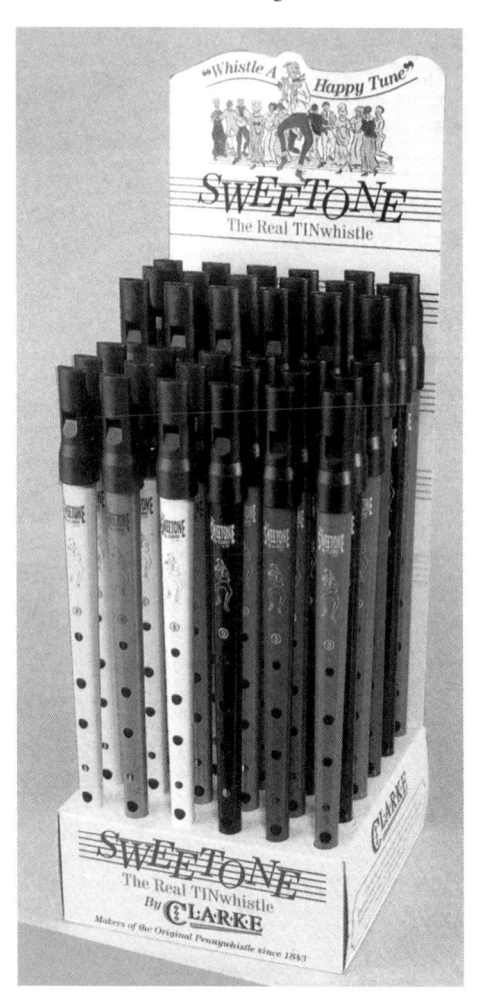

In the time of Queen Victoria there was a huge repertoire of singing games that little children sang and played in their playgrounds or in the streets. There were, of course, no cinemas, radio, TV or computer games so the children found their own amusement, in which these singing games played a large part. The tunes, by virtue of their simplicity, were easy to sing and play. The Clarke Tinwhistle, being inexpensive, was the one melodic instrument that many children could afford to own and it became

25. Enchanted Whistle

the instrument of the streets and playgrounds. I remember being taught these tunes by our teachers, singing games like "Oranges and Lemons", "Here we go round the Mulberry Bush" and "London Bridge is falling down"; and enjoying playing them in our playground. And I owned a Clarke Tinwhistle in the 1920's with which I played the tunes. With emigration in the 1800's, Clarke's Tinwhistles and Singing Games went to the USA and kept their popularity with the children, although sometimes the words changed to suit the part of the country. For example, "Here we go round the Mulberry Bush" became "Here we go round the Barberry Bush".

These days I am saddened to see children rushing around in the playground, kicking each other with the "Kung Fu" attacks they have seen on the TV, instead of playing those more innocent singing games.

26. Victorian Singing Games Tinwhistle

Jim Weedon and I decided to produce a Victorian Singing Games Tinwhistle. (Picture 26) I designed a fingering chart with a selection of Singing Games, together with their melodies arranged for easy playing on the D Tinwhistle and instructions for the performance of the dances. This could give young children some of the fun and pleasure of a bygone age and they would not only enjoy these Singing Games but they would become pleasant memories for them to carry into adulthood – as indeed they were to me.

The Sweetone occasionally appears in the USA wearing other liveries. If you were to go for a cruise down the Mississippi on one of the high stern wheelers you could purchase a Sweetone with a picture of the boat on it. You might attempt to join in playing with the boat's steam calliope. The Sweetones are also available in Yellowstone Park with a picture of a bear and the word "Yellowstone" down its length. The bear is, of course, neither Yogi Bear or Boo Boo...

Probably the favourite instrument for folk music throughout the various Celtic countries is the whistle. For them Jim has devised a Celtic Tinwhistle (Picture 27). It is lacquered a shade of emerald green with a Celtic knot as a logo. It is marketed in an attractive box decorated all over with Celtic knots and it includes a fingering chart with five tunes, one each from Scotland, Wales and Brittany and

27.
Celtic Tinwhistle

The Making of a Clarke Tinwhistle 55

28. Children playing Sweetones in Zimbabwe

two from Ireland. It has become very popular in, you've guessed it, the Celtic countries. And others for that matter! Not long ago, we had a visit in the Tinwhistle factory by Sheila Cameron from Zimbabwe. She was most enthusiastic about re-kindling interest in that country for Kwela music played on Tinwhistles. The sort of whistle, probably a Hohner whistle, that had been used in the past was no longer obtainable and she hoped that the Clarke Sweetone Tinwhistle might fill the gap and start a renaissance of Kwela music. The local musicians have a unique method of blowing their whistles. The whole of the mouthpiece is put in the mouth so that the lips cover the window. Only in this way can they get the tonal quality that Kwela whistle music requires. Unfortunately this method of blowing is not easy with a Clarke tinwhistle but Sheila hopes that the children will learn to play their traditional tunes on their Sweetones without attempting Kwela techniques. (Picture 28) We are wondering if these children will be allowed to keep the Sweetones she took to Bulawayo for them. Jim Weedon made a present of a batch of Sweetones for

29. Meg Tinwhistle

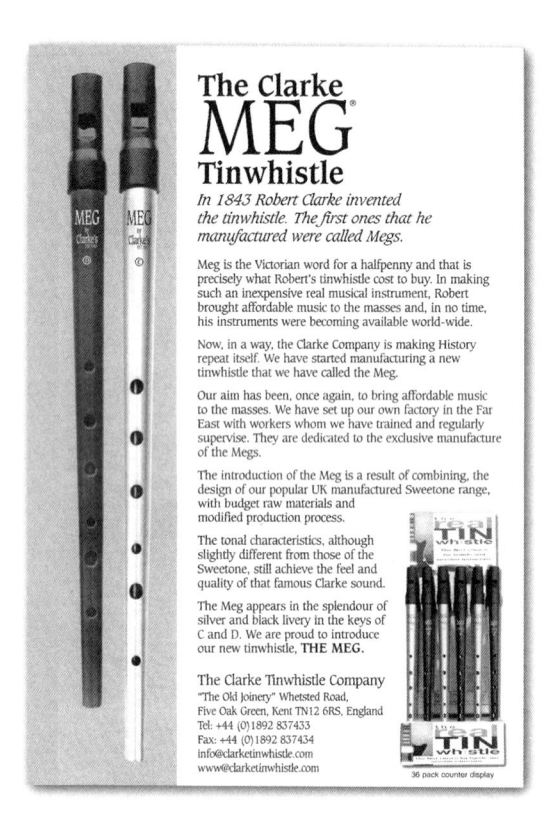

The Clarke MEG® Tinwhistle

In 1843 Robert Clarke invented the tinwhistle. The first ones that he manufactured were called Megs.

Meg is the Victorian word for a halfpenny and that is precisely what Robert's tinwhistle cost to buy. In making such an inexpensive real musical instrument, Robert brought affordable music to the masses and, in no time, his instruments were becoming available world-wide.

Now, in a way, the Clarke Company is making History repeat itself. We have started manufacturing a new tinwhistle that we have called the Meg.

Our aim has been, once again, to bring affordable music to the masses. We have set up our own factory in the Far East with workers whom we have trained and regularly supervise. They are dedicated to the exclusive manufacture of the Megs.

The introduction of the Meg is a result of combining, the design of our popular UK manufactured Sweetone range, with budget raw materials and modified production process.

The tonal characteristics, although slightly different from those of the Sweetone, still achieve the feel and quality of that famous Clarke sound.

The Meg appears in the splendour of silver and black livery in the keys of C and D. We are proud to introduce our new tinwhistle, THE MEG.

The Clarke Tinwhistle Company
"The Old Joinery" Whetsted Road,
Five Oak Green, Kent TN12 6RS, England
Tel: +44 (0)1892 837433
Fax: +44 (0)1892 837434
info@clarketinwhistle.com
www.clarketinwhistle.com

those children and they got on marvellously with them. Unfortunately, even the low price of a Sweetone made it impossible for more children to buy them. Zimbabwe has certainly become a very poor country.

In his concern that, in certain poorer countries, the price of the Tinwhistles might be too dear, Jim decided to go to China and set up a factory, where the labour and cost of raw materials was less expensive. This he achieved, using workers whom he and the Clarke factory manager, Ray Fermor, trained and regularly supervise. It was all done officially, with the blessing of the Chinese Government, ensuring that the workers were paid a proper wage.

As the first Tinwhistles came off the production line, they were sent to the English factory, where Goretti Anglim

(Picture 38) and I tested them for intonation and tonal qualities. There were slight problems at first, especially in the plastic mouthpieces, produced in a separate factory, but the efficient Chinese workers soon corrected them and produced fine instruments.

Their tonal characteristics, although slightly different from those of the Sweetone, still achieve the feel and quality of the famous Clarke sound.

All those years ago, Robert Clarke's first commercially made Tinwhistles were called Megs. Now, in a way, Jim was making history repeat itself, for he gave the name Meg to the new Chinese Tinwhistles. (Picture 29)

The new instruments are a result of combining the design of the popular UK manufactured Sweetone range of Tinwhistles with budget raw materials and a modified production process. Our Chinese workers are dedicated to the exclusive manufacture of the Megs.

In all his negotiations in China, Jim needed the help of an interpreter who could guide him through the maze of Chinese bureaucracy and enable him to talk with the workers. He found a Taiwanese lady who had a ready command of several of the Chinese dialects and could help him in setting up the paperwork. She is Hsu Hsiu Chin, a lovely person, always happy and most industrious. When a child she was called Jeanie. That makes it much easier for us to say than Hsu Hsiu Chin! As Jim got to know her well, she began to fill the sad gap that he was continually feeling over the loss of his wife, Carol. As time went on he was permitted to bring her to the UK and she now works in our factory here, where her cheerful nature and hardworking efficiency has endeared her to all of us. Jeanie has certainly brought a ray of sunshine into Jim's life and we all are delighted for him. (Picture 30)

In 2003, Jim found a new series of Tinwhistle tutor books by a German teacher named Andreas Joseph in

30. Jeanie

31. Andreas Joseph's tutor book "Tinwhistle"

the Frankfurt Music Show. I was so impressed by these books that I suggested that they should be translated into English. The outcome was that they were indeed translated by Willoughby Ann Walshe. I was involved as a music consultant, helping to make sure that all the musical nomenclature and notation would be applicable, not only to the original German readers and those influenced by American music educationalists but also to those in the sphere of British education. The Germans and Americans, for instance, say "quarter-note" when the British say

32. Liz Shropshire with Kosova homeless children

"crotchet". As George Bernard Shaw once stated, "England and America are two countries separated by a common language!"

Naturally, the Clarke Company markets the English language version. (Picture 31)

There is a wonderful American lady named Liz Shropshire. (Picture 32) She was deeply concerned about the quality of life of the war-affected children and adolescents in Kosova. She determined to do something about it using her skills, drawing on her advanced degrees in musical composition and twenty years experience in music and education.

When she arrived in Kosova she found that it was far more shocking than anything she had seen on TV. Entire villages were burned to the ground. In the rubble-filled streets, children "played executioner" with toy guns, re-enacting on each other the traumatic violence they had witnessed. The need for healing was tangible.

Liz set up her base of operations in the town of Gjakove, one of the cities hit most by ethnic cleansing. It was the site of high levels of casualties, kidnappings, evacuations, sexual abuse, destruction of homes and property, land-mining, anti-teacher militia violence and mass killings. Many of these atrocities were committed against and witnessed by the children of Gjakove.

In the Autumn of 1999, she successfully organised a short-term music programme for 300 refugee children in a secondary school and a transit shelter camp, using Tinwhistles, harmonicas, electric keyboards and supplying beginner piano books and even pencils. She solicited help from instrument manufacturers, including the Clarke Company, held fund-raising activities and emptied her own savings account. Since then her organisation has created a number of humanitarian music education programmes, reaching thousands of children in Gjakove and surrounding villages.

First of all Jim made Liz a generous offer of natural tin-plate Sweetones (Liz's own choice) but it became apparent that, owing to the high humidity and sweaty fingers, the tin-plate became tarnished. Jim immediately swapped the Sweetones for the new Megs with their black lacquer.

By 2003 Liz's organisation had benefited more than 3000 Kosovar Albanian, Serbian, and Roma children. (Picture 33)

33. Kosovar children with their Megs

Whistlers Past and Present

The Tinwhistle, although quite a humble member of the fipple flute family, nevertheless demands considerable technique if it is to be played properly. Ever since the Clarke Tinwhistle first appeared it has attracted to itself players who have mastered the skill necessary for virtuoso performance.

By all accounts, Robert Clarke himself was a fine player. George Goddard describes how Robert and George Barton used to play outside Robert's house on summer evenings. Robert played the whistle and George Barton the violin. People used to gather outside to hear the concerts.

The following collection of Tinwhistle players is, of course, by no means exhaustive. Of the living ones, these are people I have heard about and who have been in contact with me. There are many, many more I would have liked to have included, but these few appealed to me specially because of their interesting lives.

WHISTLING BILLY

One of the most charismatic whistlers of all times was Whistling Billy. (Picture 34) He is described comprehensively by Henry Mayhew in his book *London Labour and the London Poor* (1861). Mayhew's description of Billy is so graphic that one can almost see him.

He was a red-headed lad, of that peculiar white complexion which accompanies hair of that colour. His forehead was covered with freckles, so thick, that they looked as if a quantity of cayenne pepper had been sprinkled over it; and when he frowned, his hair moved backwards and forwards like the twitching of a horse shaking off flies.

Mayhew goes on to describe Billy's clothes. When he bought a new item of clothing he would haggle for it with the dealer. His shoes were in a very bad state of repair – one gaped open and had the toes sticking out. This came from doing the double shuffle when he danced. His outer garment was a washed-out linen blouse, such as glaziers wear and his trousers were of coarse canvas, stained black on the thighs.

He was not sure of his age at that time, but estimated that he was seventeen "come two months".

He was in the habit of drinking to excess, nearly always intoxicated at the end of the evening. He would insist that the drink was as food to him and it was apparent from his thin body and pinched face that this was the case.

He reckoned on earning two pounds a week which was an enormous amount of money in those times.

When quite young he used to go to Shilling Balls where he would dance for money in front of the ladies. He could get his entry fee back and have some money left over to buy sweets and some to take home to his mother

He left home, confident that he could earn his own living by dancing. Unfortunately he fell in with another boy who led him into crime. This boy persuaded him to steal the brass cock from a big water butt in a foundry. The foundry was then flooded with 150 gallons of water and Billy was later recognised by his red hair by a policeman. He got two months in 'quod' and resolved never to steal again. On coming out of jail he was given one shilling, with part of which he purchased a Clarke Tinwhistle. Henry Mayhew refers to it as a Pennywhistle – the first time I know of its receiving that name. At first he did not dance while playing, but gave the audiences in the pubs his repertoire of about six songs, including the popular songs of the day. He made eleven 'bob' (shillings) the first week he was out of prison – a lot of money.

Then he took to selling the whistles after his performance. He could get tuppence a piece for them and even as much as sixpence or a shilling. He bought them for 3d a dozen and was earning as much as 17 or 18 shillings a week doing this but found it a dull way of making money. It was then that he took up dancing to his own accompaniment on the Tinwhistle.

He travelled all around Devonshire and as far as Land's End, playing and dancing in front of hotels and spirit shops and even played for cottagers who'd given him half pennies and bread. He would often be engaged by the farmers to play at harvest suppers, for which he was paid as much as 5 shilling plus six or seven shillings given him in small change by the men.

The dances he did were hornpipes, bandy jigs and country dances. Many of the labourers were Irish so Billy built up a repertoire of Irish jigs.

The bandy jig was an ordinary Irish jig danced with his toes turned in as if he were bandy.

He toured seaside towns where there were regattas and at one stage joined a group of tumblers, with whom he learnt tumbling. For them he played the drum and the mouth-pipes.

At one time he seems to have tired of dancing and joined the crew of a fishing boat. He soon tired of this life when he found that he was not allowed to drink on board.

One of his tricks was to play the Tinwhistle up his nose, but only when he did not have a cold. He had to be careful, however,

34. Whistling Billy

because this would attract a huge crowd and then he would be in trouble with the police. Nose playing produced a quieter sound, but still strong enough to be heard "all over the house".

Despite the way in which Billy must have abused his health by continually drinking his money away, he lived to a ripe old age, still whistling and dancing. I mentioned him to Nelly Sims, a lady I know. She has been a flower seller in Romford Market since she was a girl. She became quite excited and told me that she remembered Billy as a very old man, still whistling and dancing in Romford in the early 1920's. He was allowed to perform outside certain of the pubs in the marketplace, but not others, where he was banned. He was used as a crowd puller by two men, the Strong Brothers. These two used to have a stand in the market and always stood there stripped to the waist in all weathers. Billy played and danced in front of them and attracted a large crowd. Then he would stop playing and disappear. Immediately the Strong Brothers would take over and start selling their patent medicines.

Nelly remembers how she and her young friends loved to dance to Billy's music. There were no other entertainments for young children which were so immediately obtainable and affordable! Billy also played for the Irish navvies, entertaining them with his repertoire of Irish tunes. His pièce de résistance was to play an Irish jig whilst dancing the same jig on the blade of an Irishman's shovel. He slept in a doss-house in South Street near the marketplace. Billy apparently had religious principles for he would never play for money on a Sunday. He would march and play along behind the Salvation Army band as they paraded in Romford on the way to their Citadel.

His picture adorns the Clarke Sweetone Tinwhistle.

WEE WILLIE WHITE

Wee Willie White (Picture 35) was a diminutive, blind, street performer. He is described in a book, *Glasgow Characters* by Peter Mackenzie, published in 1857. The illustration was made with little attempt at accuracy, as the whistle he is playing seems to be upside-down. I do not know of any whistle which has the smaller end of the cone in the mouth. The book describes it as either a flute or a flageolet – neither of which, I would think, is correct. Wee Willie White was said to have lived inoffensively and the money he earned by exercising his musical talents kept him in respectable poverty. He was suddenly taken ill whilst performing and died quietly soon after he was taken to his lodging on the same day. He must have been well thought of, for his admirers provided for a decent interment and marked the resting place of his body by a simple monumental stone which bears a representation of his favourite musical instrument and the box in which he always carried it.

35. Wee Willie White

JOCK MACLEAN

Jock Maclean's whole life was spent, like Whistling Billy's, as a street musician, always playing the Clarke Tinwhistle. He could be seen and heard in the streets of Glasgow. He would tell you that his father before him also followed the same profession and, more than that, *his* father before *him*. Jock had a large repertoire of tunes, and also the ability to play two Tinwhistles at the same time. He fitted a small metal cone on the end of one of his Tinwhistles, rather like the bell of a trumpet. This he would inform you, confidingly, enabled him to play in stereo. I met him at just about the time the whistle factory was transferred to Tonbridge. He demonstrated to me his skill with some pride, but complained bitterly that he could not find a shop which sold Clarke's Tinwhistles anymore. He was worried that he might not be able to replace his one when it was too old to play. I told him that not only was Clarke's Tinwhistle factory alive and well, but was also making the instruments at full production. I cheered him up by telling him that I would put two new Tinwhistles in the post for him as soon as I got back to Tonbridge but had no acknowledgement. Recently efforts have been made to trace him, to no avail. What has happened to Jock Maclean?

ROBERT LOUIS STEVENSON

When I was a child in a primary school, our teacher introduced us to the magic of Robert Louis Stevenson's stories by reading us *Treasure Island*, in instalments once a week. I was really excited by it. Little did I know that R.L.S. played the very same type of instrument as I myself played – the Tinwhistle or as it was known, both to R.L.S. and me, as the Pennywhistle.

In a letter about his children's poems to W.E. Henley (Nice, March 1883) he wrote:

❖ "O I forgot. As for the title, I think 'Nursery Verses' the best. Poetry is not the strong point of the text, and I shrink from any title that might seem to claim that quality; otherwise we might have 'Nursery Muses' or 'New Songs of Innocence' (but that were a blasphemy), or 'Rimes of Innocence': the last not bad, or – an idea – 'The Jews' Harp,' or – now I have it – 'The Penny Whistle.'

36. Robert Louis Stevenson playing a flageolet

THE PENNY WHISTLE:
NURSERY VERSES
BY ROBERT LOUIS STEVENSON.
ILLUSTRATED BY - - -

And here we have an excellent frontispiece, of a party playing on a P. W. to a little ring of dancing children.

THE PENNY WHISTLE is the name for me.
Fool! this is all wrong, here is the true name:-
PENNY WHISTLES FOR SMALL WHISTLERS.

The second title is queried, it is perhaps better, as simply PENNY WHISTLES.

Nor you, O Penny Whistler, grudge
That I your instrument debase:
By worse performers still we judge,
And give that fife a second place!
Crossed penny whistles on the cover, or else a sheaf of 'em." ❖

Unfortunately there isn't a picture of R.L.S. playing a Tinwhistle. In this picture (Picture 36) he plays a flageolet. It's the nearest I could get but, after all, the flageolet was the grandfather of the Tinwhistle. (Its father was, of course, Robert Clarke's little wooden whistle that he copied in tinplate.)

ARTHUR RANSOME

Throughout the world, generations of children have thrilled to the Swallows and Amazons stories written by Arthur Ransome (Picture 37) and have been encouraged to experience life in the adventurous spirit of the novels. As well as being a very successful author, Arthur was also an enthusiastic Pennywhistle player. He enjoyed playing the instrument together with his young friends who were playing theirs. In his biography, *The Life of Arthur Ransome* by Hugh Brogan, there is a picture of him and three young people all playing their Pennywhistles together. He even blamed a mistake in his drawing of a semaphore message in the book, *Missee Lee* on Captain Flint's carelessness, due to listening to

37. Arthur Ransome playing his Pennywhistle

Pennywhistle music. – "While he was doing it Roger was playing the Pennywhistle and somebody else was not doing any harm just fingering Captain Flint's new accordion. He says there are at least eight mistakes in the signals. Really of course his beastly carelessness." The mistakes were pointed out to Arthur by an observant Brownies patrol.

Many years ago, Gabriel Woolf, I believe it was, played his Pennywhistle at the start and end of his recording for radio of Arthur's *We didn't mean to go to Sea*. On another occasion, the Arthur Ransome Society took a number of their Youth Club and other fans to take part in filming the BBC Bookworm programme on Arthur Ransome at Pin Mill. When not being filmed they all whipped out their Pennywhistles and began playing. The BBC tried to film them doing it but, due to their never having played together before, the shots were not satisfactory and, sadly, were not used.

GORETTI ANGLIM

Goretti (Picture 38) was born into a family steeped in Irish Traditional Music. Her maternal grandmother played the fiddle and her paternal grandmother taught Irish dancing to all her children and accompanied this on the concertina. Her father, Richard Ryan of Coolacussane in Co. Tipperary, was a well-known fiddler and was successful in the All Ireland Competitions in the 1950's. It was he who gave Goretti her first Tinwhistle, a Clarke's. She also plays a simple system Gerok 18th Century flute and a Miller and Weeks Boehm system 1980 flute.

Her elder daughter, Carline, was winner of the All Ireland Fiddle Championship and the BBC Radio 2 Young Tradition Award, at the age of sixteen. Her son, Richard, plays drums, guitar and bodhran. The younger daughter, Sorcha, still at school, is already shining at both Tinwhistle and fiddle.

Goretti is valued greatly by the Clarke Company for her expert advice on the continual quality of the Tinwhistles.

38. Goretti Anglim

MARY BERGIN

At the age of nine Mary Bergin (Picture 39) was encouraged to take up a musical instrument. She had been born into a very musical family and took to music quite naturally. Her first instrument was a Clarke Tinwhistle, which she learnt to play almost on her own, practising daily at the back of the school bus on the way to and from school. Due to her own dedication, and with the encouragement of her family, she developed a highly original and innovatory style of playing which re-defined what Tinwhistle playing is all about. By her late teens she had won the All-Ireland Championship.

She has the reputation of being Ireland's premier exponent on the Tinwhistle. Her solo album Feadóga Stáin, brought out in 1979, holds its place as a classic in latter-day traditional music.

39. Mary Bergin

Many consider it to be the finest recording of Tinwhistle playing ever made. A large portion of the recording is devoted to medleys of jigs and reels played with dazzling virtuosity and skill.

In 1990, Mary together with Kathleen Louhnane on the harp and Dearbhbaill Standúb on the fiddle formed a group called Dordán. Mary features a variety of whistles and the wooden flute. The group plays a large range of music from traditional Irish tunes to music from the Baroque period. The word Dordán evokes a happy image of pleasant murmurings, like that of the sea or a hive of honeybees.

The first recording together of Dordán presents an intriguing and highly personal selection of music, ranging in mood from the delicacy and sensitivity of a chamber trio to the vigorous attack characteristic of traditional musicians. The three of them did, in fact, first meet and are best known as traditional musicians.

Mary's life is devoted to the promotion and dissemination of traditional music. She performs widely – as soloist; with Dordán; and with Antoinette and Joe McKenna. Antoinette, Mary's sister, plays the harp and Joe plays the Uilleann pipes. Mary is utterly committed to imparting her skills to others: her multi-faceted teaching schedule includes a regular system of music classes in the Spiddal area in the Irish speaking part of West Co. Galway where she lives. She travels extensively to conduct workshops and seminars; and – a recent innovation in her teaching regime because of the increasing international appeal of her music – she provides tuition through correspondence to pupils all over the world.

Mary has won many awards in Oireachtas and Fleadh Ceoil competitions, including the All-Ireland Championships at Junior and Senior levels. She has toured extensively in Europe, in America and in Australia, performing on radio and television wherever she visited. In 1989 she performed in Moscow and Leningrad with an invited group of Irish musicians. She has returned on a number of occasions to Helsinki, where she has been guest artist at a major folk music festival.

Mary has given masterclasses in Britain (1989 and 1993), and, in Australia, at Melbourne University and in Perth, in a visit sponsored by the Department of External Affairs (1984). She was also invited to perform at Sweden's largest International Folk Festival.

40. Adrian Brett

ADRIAN BRETT

At the beginning of December 1993, the music for a film about Wyatt Earp called *Tombstone* was recorded by the Sinfonia of London. The second flute player was Adrian Brett. (Picture 40) He found that there was a part for the Tinwhistle in his score. He rummaged in his bag and produced a somewhat battered Clarke Tinwhistle in an earlier livery. The bassoonist sitting near to him, Ian Cuthill, introduced himself as a descendant of the original Clarke family. Adrian told Ian "My Clarke Tinwhistle is the best".

ROGER BUCKTON

Dr. Buckton (Picture 41) is a New Zealander. He is a recorder player of considerable merit and plays modern, Baroque and Renaissance flutes as a soloist. He is also an educationalist with a great enthusiasm for the use of the recorder as a means of giving the children a well-rounded musical education. To this end he has written a series of progressive recorder tutors which is gaining success throughout the world. Recently he has been involved in the New Zealand Music Syllabus Revision Committee and the associated "think tank". He gives flute and recorder recital concerts with a guitarist and, just before the interval, he puts his flutes and recorders down and takes up the Tinwhistle, giving his audiences a brilliant exposition of that instrument, playing a collection of (mostly) Irish tunes. He really enjoys playing the Clarke Tinwhistle and says that it makes a delightful way of finishing the first half of his concerts.

41. Roger Buckton

42. James Galway playing his Clarke Pennywhistle at the launch of the Mourne Mountains Appeal

JAMES GALWAY

James Galway (Picture 42) has a world-wide reputation for his exceptional flute playing and has played with the great orchestras as lead flautist and also as concerto soloist.

As a child in his home city of Belfast, Northern Ireland, his musical pilgrimage began with his playing the Clarke Tinwhistle.

He has gained a tremendous reputation in recent years for his work in encouraging children to make music. He attaches a great deal of importance to this work. Recently, on the foothills of Slieve Donard, he launched the £350,000 Mourne Mountains appeal for the National Trust, which had purchased Slieve Donard, the highest peak in the Mournes. James often speaks of his love for the area and therefore had no hesitation in accepting the position of appeal President, in which position he is determined not to be a mere figurehead. At the launch, typically, he appeared with four youngsters who played their flutes whilst he played his Clarke Tinwhistle. More recently he appeared on TV's *Blue Peter* with a large group of children all playing their flutes, but that time he played his flute.

James Galway made a special appearance in the TV film about the life of Robert Clarke made by Malachite for the 150th Anniversary of the first Tinwhistle. For that occasion, he composed and played a lively Tinwhistle tune which he named "Mr. Clarke's Jig".

WILL HASTIE

Will Hastie (Picture 43) was born in Lanarkshire, Scotland and learnt to play the Clarke Tinwhistle at an early age; the traditional music of his homeland, namely strathspeys and reels etc., provided him with an abiding interest.

The Clan or Family 'Hastie' is listed in the Oxford Companion to Music as being a famous family of Scottish bagpipers. Will is no exception and won medals for piping in various competitions while still a schoolboy at Lanark.

Always a keen jazz fan, he switched to clarinet and made his way south to London to play with such famous bands as Freddy Randall, Al Fairweather, Kenny Ball, Allan Bradley's All Stars, and Keith Nichol's Ragtime Orchestra.

43. Will Hastie

Both Keith Nichols and Allan Bradley have featured Will on their records playing his Tinwhistle.

But perhaps it would be true to say that he is best known for his work with the Temperance Seven, of which he has been a regular member for nigh on thirty years.

His sense of humour and fun is also well known. Whilst en route to Bahrain to play an engagement with the Temperance Seven, he played his Tinwhistle on board Concord, so he can honestly claim to have played the Tinwhistle at twice the speed of sound!

DES LANE

Des Lane (Picture 44) is by way of being a latter-day Whistling Billy, in that he whistles and dances just like Billy used to do. However, unlike that much-maligned vagabond, Des is a highly respected member of the theatrical profession.

He tells me that he cannot remember ever not playing the Pennywhistle, as he always called it. His father was a Pennywhistle player – the Clarke of course – and he must have put his instrument into the hands of the tiny Des at a very tender age. Des was encouraged to play, especially by his mother. When he was three or four years old, she would give him a ha'penny every time he played *Moonlight and Roses* – her favourite piece.

44 . Des Lane

He inherited the ability to dance whilst playing from his uncle (his Irish uncle, indeed) who played the fife and danced reels and other Irish dances at the same time.

He first went on the stage at the age of fifteen. At that time he was in the Air Training Corps. A show was arranged by the entertainments officer, who detailed members of the corps with any talent at all to perform. Des was pushed, unwilling and nervous, onto the stage to give a violin solo. After that, as they say, he never looked back!

Over the years he has developed his own highly individualistic style of entertainment: Pennywhistle, jazz-clarinet, dancing and improvised chats with the audience – all put over in an engaging and exuberant way.

Des has performed in Variety, Cabaret, Pantomime, on board cruise ships, on Decca and Top Rank discs and on TV; and has starred with a great number of the leading artists of the Theatre – people like Bruce Forsyth, Val Doonican,

Lena Horne, Gracie Fields, Shirley Bassey, Max Bygraves, Cliff Richard and Tom Jones, to mention just a few. He has played four seasons at the London Palladium, the ultimate accolade for a variety artiste.

He is an original entertainer with an enviable reputation among his fellow performers – stars and otherwise – as an absolute Show-Stopper.

James Green of the *Evening News* once wrote of him that he comes on stage like a white tornado (he always appears in white clothes) and does an audience warm up that belongs to the Guinness Book of Records. Within seconds he has the whole audience stomping like a private party and whether playing or dancing he is always rewarded with waves of applause.

It is no wonder that he is internationally acclaimed as "The Pennywhistle Man".

LES LIEBER

Les Lieber (Picture 45) is a public relations consultant, which he considers his "real profession", but it seems that he has a strong and affectionate leaning to his other "profession" – that of jazz Tinwhistle player.

He was born in St. Louis in 1912 and took up the saxophone at the age of 13. A few years later he heard a record called *Piccolo Pete* played by Ted Weems' Orchestra and upon learning that the piccolo solo was, in fact, played on a Tinwhistle he rushed over to the music store and purchased a Clarke Pennywhistle. From then on, as he puts it, he has never left home without a Tinwhistle in his inside jacket pocket.

His first job was as a feature writer in the publicity department of the Columbia Broadcasting System. In 1936, they launched a national jazz programme called *The Saturday Night*

45. Les Lieber

Swing Session which featured all the great soloists of the day – Benny Goodman, Artie Shaw, Tommy Dorsey, Bunny Berrigan, Duke Ellington's Men, etc. He appeared 17 times as a guest on that programme.

In 1937 he left CBS to handle the publicity for Paul Whiteman, then the most celebrated orchestra leader in the states. In addition to his regular press work, he appeared twice as Tinwhistle player on Whiteman's coast-to-coast radio show, playing complicated half jazz, purposely concert-sounding arrangements with the symphonic 35-piece aggregation behind him – first *The Parade of the Wooden Soldiers* (complete with opening cadenza) and, two weeks later, *Nola*.

In 1938, with Whiteman in semi-retirement, he became Benny Goodman's PR man and had the extra bonus of appearing as a Tinwhistle player on the Benny Goodman Sextet appearances.

During the War (having sneaked a soprano saxophone and five Tinwhistles in his duffel bag) he served overseas in the 9th Air Force Service Command and towards the end of the War he became director of publicity for the American Forces Network. During this period he made it his business to seek out the famous guitar player, Django Reinhart of The Hot Club de Paris fame. Reinhart's whereabouts had been unknown since the outbreak of War but Les found him and bought him to the AFN Studios in Paris. There he made a record, playing the Tinwhistle, with Reinhart. This record still exists and can be found in specialist jazz record shops.

After the War, he continued to play the Tinwhistle for his own amusement, but from time to time he appeared on well-known TV shows and in jazz clubs would saunter uninvited onto the stage to take a couple of choruses with whichever group was playing. But only if they were playing in a good key for his Tinwhistle.

He became a magazine writer and that, not Tinwhistle playing, became his consuming career – writing between 450 and 500 articles for a national magazine – almost none of them about music!

Regretting the fact that he and myriads of other jazz

instrumentalists in the business world who, when in college, could have been in orchestras and could no longer have such an opportunity, he started an event called Jazz at Noon with a nucleus of advertising men, doctors, lawyers and business executives who had been or could have been jazz musicians. Now, years later, they meet every Friday in a New York restaurant, and have become the longest lasting jazz event in that city and attract a goodly crowd for Friday lunch.

There is, of course, a Tinwhistle solo each week by, as he says, "guess who?"

TOMMY MAKEM

Bill Ochs first heard Tommy Makem (Picture 46) playing in 1960 and was immediately hooked. Bill says that Tommy played his Pennywhistle with the verve of a fife or a piccolo.

Tommy Makem is the champion Irish tinwhistle player. He is also a fine singer with a dark, husky baritone voice; a storyteller; an actor and a songwriter. He also plays the banjo.

46. Tommy Makem

As the son of the legendary song collector and folk singer Sarah Makem he grew up surrounded by songs going back into the earliest mists of Irish history.

He started playing a Clarke Tinwhistle in Keady, Co. Armagh, back in the early 1940's. He cannot remember how much they cost in those days – either tenpence or one shilling and sixpence.

His older brother, Jack, had two of them that he kept on top of the dresser in the kitchen. He kept pestering his brother until he finally gave in and showed him how to play the scale; and it seemed to him that he was in heaven.

Shortly after that he saved up

enough money to buy his own Tinwhistle and he carried it in his inside jacket pocket wherever he went.

By the time he was seventeen, Tommy had taken to the stage and was the star performer with the Keady Dramatic Society. He won acting awards at drama festivals all over Ireland and received many invitations to turn professional. As if that were not enough, he was also the lead singer with the Clippertones Showband, whistle player in the local ceili band, lead baritone in his church choir, and a piper in the local pipe band.

Like all struggling young artists, Tommy needed a "day" job to keep, as he says, "his ribs from poking through his chest". He became a clerk in a garage in Keady.

In 1956 he emigrated to the United States, and settled in Dover, New Hampshire where he worked in a factory, but a cruel accident perversely forced him to take the first leap towards international stardom. His left hand was crushed and he could no longer work in the factory. Yet this made him free to take off for New York where he met up with Liam, Pat and Tom Clancy. He also established himself with a brief but frenetically successful career on live TV, Summer Stock and Off-Broadway.

He was starting out on what has become a life-time as a professional folk singer and was about to record his first LP with the folk group called The Clancy Brothers and Tommy Makem; and his Clarke Tinwhistle was a very important part of that recording. That was in 1956. He believes that he was the first folk musician to use a tinwhistle on a commercial recording. And it was a Clarke!

In 1961 he appeared in the Newport Folk Festival where he and Joan Baez were honoured as the most promising newcomers on the folk music scene.

After that he was in as much demand as a singer as he was as an actor. Together with the Clancy Brothers, Tommy played to packed houses around the world; Carnegie Hall in New York; Royal Albert Hall in London; Boston's Symphony Hall and the Sydney Opera House.

The Clancy Brothers and Tommy Makem became the most famous Irishmen in the world in a phenomenon that was even bigger than Beatlemania for its sheer intensity.

Tommy left the Clancy Brothers in 1969 to establish a solo singing career with sell-out performances in the Carnegie Hall followed by great successes in Australia, Ireland and Great Britain. He also found time for TV series for Scottish Television, BBC Belfast, Ulster Television, CHCH-TV Hamilton, Ontario, CBC Vancouver and several one-hour specials for Radio Telefís Eireann in Dublin.

In 1975 he met up again with Liam Clancy and joined him in a short performance which was rewarded by a standing ovation that went on for five minutes. This led to their working together for many years – records and concert tours, including an award-winning series from Calgary, Alberta and another for New Hampshire public television that was nominated for an Emmy.

In 1987 Tommy was honoured with a gold medal from the Eire society of Boston for his contribution to Irish culture. *Irish America Magazine* named him one of the top 100 Irish-Americans. And the description is accurate, for in September 1987, Tommy Makem, the latter-day Bard of Armagh, raised his hand and became an American citizen.

He still possesses two or three of the old Clarke Tinwhistles at home and had been keeping them safely tucked away thinking that the Clarke Tinwhistle Company were out of business, until a few years ago when he was talking to Bill Ochs in New York and learned of the new management.

He considers that the Clarke "C" is still the sweetest sound of all the whistles available down the years.

He is still touring and performs as a solo artist; and, when he wrote to me, he was in the middle of a concert tour of the Atlantic Provinces of Canada. I later saw him on the stage of the Barbican Theatre during an Irish Festival doing his celebrated act of singing, playing his banjo, telling stories and playing his whistle. Unfortunately I had to leave the theatre early so I missed meeting him in person. That is a treat to look forward to in the future, I hope.

TIM MOON

Tim Moon (Picture 47) was born in Halifax. He first played in public at the age of 5 as a piano duettist. He is now a freelance musician with a bit of writing and drawing thrown in. As well as the Clarke Tinwhistle, he plays flutes, saxophones, panpipes, South American pipes, bombard, recorders, piano, organ, synth, all guitars, bass, banjos, mandolin, mandocello, bouzouki, cittern, dulcimer, autoharp, zither, percussion and drums, accordian, concertina, fiddle, harmonica and he does vocals. Phew! When I first met him he was working as composer/lyricist/performer in a street performance duo with the Third Theatre Company.

When the Malachite Television Film *Clarke's Pennywhistle* was produced, Tim was auditioned and chosen for the part of Robert Clarke.

47. Tim Moon as Robert Clarke in the film *Clarke's Pennywhistle*

BILL OCHS

Bill Ochs (Picture 48) was born in Newark, New Jersey in 1946. No-one in his family had ever played or even heard of the Tinwhistle as it was not part of their cultural background. They had emigrated to the U.S. around 1900 from Eastern Europe.

He told me that he first heard the Pennywhistle played by Tommy Makem of the group The Clancy Brothers and Tommy Makem and says that his soul was whisked away on hearing it.

From 1971 to 1973 he made his living by playing and selling Clarke Pennywhistles as well as bamboo flutes of his own manufacture. He can, perhaps, be described as another latter-day Whistling Billy as his story so much echoes Billy's own story. (As he admits, he was much "inspired" by the example of Whistling Billy.)

They were wonderful times while they lasted. The magic of catching people unawares and unexpected with a joyful

Pennywhistle tune is something which he always cherishes and he finds that the response to the music was always overwhelmingly warm and positive.

All except the police! Although he had a pedlar's licence, in New York City even licensed pedlars are restricted to areas in which there are basically few customers. Any major commercial district is strictly off limits but this is precisely where most pedlars operate. This is where people come to shop and spend money. He played a "cat and mouse" game with the police. Unlike other pedlars he was an easy target as, in order to advertise his product, he had to play it. Especially, playing the Pennywhistle up in the "piccolo" range immediately gave away his presence to the police. A number of times he was hauled off to the police station, given a summons and had his goods confiscated. (He thinks that, to this day, there must be some vintage Clarke Pennywhistles cached away in a police warehouse in Long Island City.)

However, he'll tell you with some pride that, among his Tinwhistle students he has had a member of the 'Pedlar Squad' police, and several policemen and ex-policemen have studied with him.

By Christmas of 1973 he was so disheartened by the situation in New York that he went to Boston to sell his wares. He had two duffel bags full of Pennywhistles which he dragged onto the train at Penn Station, New York. His friends in Boston laughed when they saw how many whistles he had bought and thought he would never sell them.

But on the Saturday before Christmas at Harvard Square in Cambridge, he sold 240 Pennywhistles in just under 4 hours – that's one a minute! People were amazed that something so inexpensive could make such lovely music. The weekdays were slower – it was so cold that he had to wear gloves with finger tips cut off so that he could still play – but by the end of the week he had sold every Pennywhistle that he had bought. Over 700 in total! As he so succinctly puts it: "I returned home much lighter – duffel bags empty,

48. Bill Ochs

but pockets full of pieces of green paper with pictures of U.S. Presidents and numbers on them".

He has become a great authority on the performance on the Uilleann pipes, having made three trips from his native New York to Ireland to study at the Willie Clancy Summer School; and having studied under leading piping teachers in Ireland and the U.S.A.

The main focus of his activities is teaching both the Tinwhistle and the Uilleann pipes. He has a number of students, most of them adults, who have a keen interest in Irish folk music as a hobby. For some time he has been putting on a hands-on workshop called "Pennywhistle Magic", but because some people would turn up thinking that he was a conjurer about to pull rabbits out of a hat, he changed the name to "Let's play the Pennywhistle". Two thirds of the programme is devoted to teaching the participants to play a simple tune on the Pennywhistle and the rest of the programme consists of playing the Pennywhistle himself and demonstrating other related folk flutes from around the world. This programme he does in schools and libraries throughout the greater New York area.

He founded the Pennywhistler's Press in 1988 with the idea of becoming a "niche publisher" of materials of interest to players of the Tinwhistle. He has published the definitive tutor for the Clarke Pennywhistle which, together with its progressive demonstration tape played by himself, became an overnight success.

Recently Bill has published a new version of his tutor, which includes a CD instead of the tape and, even more recently, a smaller version of the tutor, *Pennywhistle for Beginners* also with CD. He tells me that this is already being prepared for translation into Japanese and possibly other languages!

He keeps in touch with his many fans and customers on the Internet at www.pennywhistle.com

As mentioned before, Jim Weedon owes a debt of gratitude to Bill Ochs for his help and encouragement in the early days; and for his expertise in testing and proving the first Tinwhistles and subsequent models which he made.

MICHO RUSSELL

Micho Russell (Picture 49) was once described by the *Geo Magazine* as being "as much a tourist attraction as the Cliffs of Moher". The Irish Tourist Board featured his picture on its 1984 brochure cover along with the Book of Kells and the High Cross at Clonmacnoise. Folklorists have collected over 500 tunes and songs from him, but the most telling story is this: a young well-wisher from the Continent once sent him a card addressed simply "Micho, Ireland" – and the Post Office knew exactly where to deliver it! By the next post!

He lived at Doolin, County Clare and was Ireland's "whistling ambassador" and perhaps her best-loved traditional musician. In Japan, folk artists of his stature are formally honoured as "National Living Treasures". Although Ireland has no such official designation, Micho's contribution to the national heritage is deeply appreciated by all who know her culture.

49. Micho Russell

He started to play the Clarke Tinwhistle at the age of 11 years. He says that he did not know what attracted him to the Tinwhistle as it was all concertina playing in his part of Ireland. An old man began to teach him on a little rusty whistle, smaller than the Clarke ones. Could it have been an early Clarke Meg? He found it difficult to learn. The man showed him which fingers to lift, but, as he put it, "he would tell me such a thing in the night, and I would have it lost in the morning." He seems to have found out how to play eventually by himself. He reckoned that it is like serving an apprenticeship to a trade – you must have a foundation or a plan. This is "to cover the fingers proper"; "no matter how good you are you should not forget the scale"; "if you are playing a long time your wind-pipe will work automatically" and "posture means a lot". He admires the work of the tinwhistlers in the "old days" – men like Myles O'Maley, considering them to be in some way like philosophers or artists.

Just what was it that made Micho (pronounced "Mike-O") so special?

Undeniably, his style of playing the Pennywhistle was unique for its charm and sweetness. His musical repertoire redounded with rare and unusual pieces acquired in the pre-gramophone days of the early 20th Century. He was also a great singer of songs, teller of tales and, at nearly 80, still spry enough to get up and dance a "double batter" when the spirit moved him.

Yet as much an anything else, it was Micho's genial persona which endeared him to his audience. A farmer who "got swept up" in the folk music revival of the 1960's he remained quite unaffected by celebrity and attention.

In his checked cap and rural attire, Micho was as relaxed on stage in front of thousands as he was in front of his own turf fire. Indeed, he would seem to bring something of the intimate atmosphere of the turf fire with him wherever he went. Anyone who knows Irish culture realises immediately that here was a great original, someone whose very words and mannerisms were to be savoured. Audiences invariably left a Micho Russell performance totally enchanted.

In November 1990, Micho made his first solo tour of the United States, performing for three weeks up and down the east coast. He flew to the States again in June 1992 to headline the Irish Festival at Snug Harbor, Staten Island, and returned to New York in November 1993 to do a few gigs and have "a bit of a holiday."

Though well into his seventies, Micho played with as much joy and sparkle as ever. He charmed audiences on each of these visits and made many new fans and friends.

On his last trip to the United States in 1993, Micho seemed to have more energy than on previous visits – a result of dietary changes and exercise. When he boarded the Aer Lingus jet at the end of his stay, it seemed as through Ireland's "whistling ambassador" would keep going strong right up into the twenty-first century. But sadly it was not to be.

On Saturday, February 19th, 1994, while returning from a party in Spiddal, Co. Galway, Micho decided he wanted to make a phone call about something he had left behind. As the car in which he was a passenger turned into a filling station, it was hit by an oncoming vehicle. Micho died two hours later in University College Hospital, Galway.

No words could describe the atmosphere in O'Connor's Pub that night when Micho's friends and neighbours got the news. A pall of silence descended on the place. Within hours calls started to pour in from round the world – so great was the network of people who loved Micho. By Tuesday the population of Doolin had swelled to many times its normal winter size as friends and admirers came to pay their last respects to the beloved minstrel. After a beautiful requiem mass, Micho was laid to rest amid lashing wind and rain. He would have been seventy-nine years old in five weeks.

We are indeed fortunate that Bill Ochs was able to make recordings, both video and audio, of Micho during his visits to the United States and these are now obtainable through Bill's company, the Pennywhistler's Press. They are some of the last recordings that Micho ever made and the vitality of his music is astonishing. A fitting memorial to a wonderful old Irish musician.

49. Micho Russell

MICHAEL TUBRIDY

Michael Tubridy (Picture 50) grew up in West Clare, Ireland in a farming community. He says that every household in the locality had some Tinwhistles and they were always Clarke's. Many of the children would be able to play a few tunes.

His brother played the pipes in a local bagpipe band. Michael soon found that he could play the same tunes on his Tinwhistle, on the bottom octave. Later he discovered that the instrument had a definite second octave and that he could play those tunes "higher up". Looking back he thinks that that discovery was very important and it gave him great satisfaction at the time.

50. Michael Tubridy

The experience of playing the Tinwhistle enabled him to be accepted as a member of the pipe band even though he was under age. Chanters for practising pipe music were very expensive so he and his friends improvised by cutting a thumb hole at the back of a Clarke Pennywhistle to simulate the chanter fingering.

He often had to feed the calves in a distant field after school. He always took his Tinwhistle along with him and when the job was done he would sit under a haystack and play the instrument. As he played, the cows in the next field would slowly congregate in a line at the fence facing him, and there they would remain just chewing the cud and looking straight at him.

He began to play with other Tinwhistle players and to swap tunes with them. They played at house dances, with concertina and fiddle players. Many of the old concertinas were pitched in the key of C, so he could play together with them on his C Clarke.

On Saint Stephen's Day (Boxing Day) there would be a festival when a group of people in various disguises would visit the houses in the locality, singing, dancing and playing their instruments which were usually Clarke Tinwhistles and bodhrans (hand drums).

In the mid-fifties he left home and went to London, where he bought a flute for 30 shillings in Petticoat Lane. This he plays to this day. Whenever he plays the whistle, it is always the Clarke Tinwhistle in preference to all other makes.

In the sixties and the seventies, he was a member of the popular Irish folk group The Chieftains, the Clarke Tinwhistle always being featured in their concerts and albums.

A few years ago, whilst directing a group touring the East Coast of the USA, he had one item of the programme which featured six members of the group playing a selection on Clarke Tinwhistles.

At present he is organising a group of young musicians who play and sing during the Mass in their local church. When he plays with them, he always uses his old battered and much travelled Clarke Tinwhistle, regardless of what the others are playing.

DALE WISELY

Dale Wisely (Picture 51) is a minor celebrity among whistlers, and a most unlikely one at that. Dale, a middle-aged psychologist in Birmingham, Alabama, purchased his first whistle, a Clarke original Tinwhistle, in 1994.

51. Dale Wisely on the right with Jim Weedon and me

He became, by his own admission, "obsessed" with the instrument. He developed a website about whistles, which has grown into the largest and most comprehensive Internet presence devoted to whistles and whistling. Chiff & Fipple (chiffandfipple.com) now has approximately 3000 subscribers, a wealth of information about whistles, and a very busy on-line forum for those who play the whistle, the wooden flute, the Uilleann pipes, and more.

Many other names are associated with the Tinwhistle:

The distinguished conductor and pianist, Ezra Rachlin, as a young man, played the Tinwhistle. He owned a collection of Tinwhistles. One of his achievements, which he was always rightly proud of, was to give a performance of Mozart's Concerto in C for Flute and Orchestra on the Tinwhistle.

The late Billy Cotton appeared on stage with his band on TV shows and would have his Tinwhistle sticking out of his pocket. He would sometimes conduct his band with it and would often play a little solo on it to finish the performance.

Several groups of musicians have featured the Tinwhistle as a solo instrument; The Dubliners, The Spinners and Steeleye Span, to mention just a few.

Ian Cuthill, the bassoonist, whom I mentioned in connection with Adrian Brett (Picture 38) is proud of his Clarke family history. His mother, May Cuthill (née Clarke) had her 100th Birthday in December 2004. A greetings card was signed by all the members of the Tinwhistle factory and sent to her, together with a Clarke Tinwhistle, for old times sake.

A retired headteacher I know, Helen Penny, took a music degree at Cork University, for which she was required to choose an Irish folk instrument and learn to play it. She chose the Tinwhistle. Paulette Gershen, a graduate in ethnomusicology, who is also a player and lover of the

Tinwhistle, wrote to me from California for help in her research on Tinwhistles for her Master's thesis. This must mean, that all these years later Robert Clarke's humble Tinwhistle has achieved academic respectability....

Oliver Postgate, (Picture 52) the distinguished maker of children's films for the TV, played the Tinwhistle as a child. When he first made *The Clangers*, he sought a suitable sound for those little persons with which they could converse. He tried his Tinwhistle but it did not sound Clangerish enough and, although I was able to compose the score of his musical version of *Noggin the Nog*, I could suggest nothing better. He finally hit on the Swanee Whistle and that became the definitive Clangers' voice (he even made a smaller version for Tiny Clanger).

52. Oliver Postgate holding the Clangers' world; with his Clangers

Ah well! I suppose the Swanee Whistle can be looked upon as a distant but wayward cousin of the Tinwhistle!

To celebrate the 150th Anniversary of the Clarke Pennywhistle in 1993, a folk festival was held in Coney Weston, the village where it all started. Tinwhistle players from Great Britain and other parts of the world came there to honour the memory of the founder, Robert Clarke. Mary Bergin came from Ireland and gave master classes to experienced whistlers; Bill Ochs came from the United States and took classes of beginners; Mark Moggy taught bodhran playing and there were demonstrations by musical instrument makers. In the evening Mary Bergin gave a scintillating concert and was later joined by Bill

Ochs and Mark Moggy for a grand finale. Children from surrounding villages put on a dramatic presentation about Robert Clarke's life and times. The Malachite Film and Television Production Company made a film for television about Robert Clarke's life and work, starring Tim Moon as Robert Clarke. There is an uncanny likeness between Tim and the early photographs we have of Robert Clarke. Some of the shots for the film were made at Coney Weston during the festival featuring, amongst others, Mary Bergin, Bill Ochs and the South African whistler, Robert Sithole. An exhibition of early Clarke Tinwhistles and his original machinery was held in the Moyse Museum in nearby Bury St. Edmunds.

The final cachet, to crown the occasion, Jim Weedon was told that the Clarke Company had won a Business Sponsorship Incentive Scheme Award, which was presented to him by the Minister for the Arts.

Envoi

The Clarke Tinwhistles have a bright future. Apart from the continual demand for them by individual players from all over the world, Tinwhistle playing is increasingly being taught to children in schools. In fact, it has been so for many years in Ireland. Goretti Anglim (Picture 38) owes her skill on the Tinwhistle to her teacher, Dennis O'Dwyer, when she was a child in Donaskeigh Village School. (Picture 53) She now teaches children,

53. Children in Donaskeigh Village School, Ireland

54. Goretti Anglim teaching beginners in St. Mary's RC Primary School, Hornchurch

herself, to play the Tinwhistle at St. Mary's RC Primary School. (Picture 54)

A fascinating new project has opened in Berkshire. It is the South Hill Park's Traditional Music Academy. (Picture 55) Its main aim is to foster awareness, knowledge, understanding and appreciation of our heritage through the traditional arts and to promote interest and involvement in all aspects of the genre among young people across Berkshire.

It is significant that Luke Daniels, a former BBC Young Tradition Award Winner, received funding from the National Foundation for Youth Music, to enable him to visit primary schools across the region to lead Tinwhistle workshops and find gifted children whose musical ability had not flourished within the standard musical curriculum.

Those young children are then given the opportunity to learn to play a range of instruments including mandolin, harp, fiddle, bagpipes, concertina and, of course, the Tinwhistle. The classes take place at South Hill Park Arts Centre in Berkshire.

Typically, Jim Weedon offered his help as soon as he heard of the project and Clarke Tinwhistles feature in it.

55. The South Hills Traditional Music Academy Project

Tinwhistles are virtually unknown in Brazil. Folk music is played on wood or bamboo fipple flutes in the North and Northeast regions and recorder playing has deep roots in other parts. However a lady in Campinas has a positively missionary zeal in introducing Tinwhistle playing to her country. She is Marcia Contador. (Picture 56) As well as Brazilian folk tunes, she has an enormous repertoire of all sorts of music that she plays on her collection of Clarke Tinwhistles. It ranges from 12th Century Hildegard von Bingen's *Kyrie eleison,* through Burt Bacharach's *Raindrops are falling,* to modern Pop music and, of course, English, Irish and Scottish folk tunes. In fact she plays any sort of music she likes on the Tinwhistle. Lacking a backing group at present, she plays along with CDs and she gives regular recitals in her church. I have heard her play and she really does it superbly! The best way of encouraging Tinwhistle

56. Marcia Contador teaching seven-year-old Luisa

57. The Clarke Team, 2005

playing is by teaching it to children and she proves this with her young pupils who all play enthusiastically. As she puts it, "I love the Clarke Tinwhistles and whoever gets in touch with me and has the 'right feeling' for it will be contaminated by this lovely virus."

The staff of the factory (Picture 57), proud of the Tinwhistles they are making and dedicated to keeping up the high quality of production, will continue to supply all the customers world-wide with their favourite instruments.

❖ ❖ ❖

That which Robert Clarke began in 1843 marches on, today and well into the years to come.